## *"Maura! Watch out!" Spencer shouted.*

Maura wasn't altogether sure what happened next, but seconds later she was sprawling on her back on the dusty ground with Spencer on top of her.

Spencer slowly eased away from her, breathing hard.

"Are you completely and utterly mad? Red, do you know how close those hooves came to that pretty little head of yours?"

"They weren't that close," she protested, refusing to acknowledge he was right. "And don't call me Red."

"I'll call you Red if I damn well feel like it."

Outraged, she opened her mouth to protest. But her words were forgotten when her gaze collided with his. When he slowly began to lower his mouth toward hers, her pulse went into overdrive.

"Don't you dare—" she began.

"Oh, I dare," Spencer said huskily. "You know, Red, I've wanted to do this from the first moment I set eyes on you." With that, he covered her mouth with his.

Dear Reader,

Not only is February the month for lovers, it is the second month for readers to enjoy exciting celebratory titles across all Silhouette series. Throughout 2000, Silhouette Books will be commemorating twenty years of publishing the best in contemporary category romance fiction. This month's Silhouette Romance lineup continues our winning tradition.

Carla Cassidy offers an emotional VIRGIN BRIDES title, in which a baby on the doorstep sparks a second chance for a couple who'd once been *Waiting for the Wedding*—their own!—and might be again.... Susan Meier's charming miniseries BREWSTER BABY BOOM continues with *Bringing Up Babies*, as black sheep brother Chas Brewster finds himself falling for the young nanny hired to tend his triplet half siblings.

A beautiful horse trainer's quest for her roots leads her to two men in Moyra Tarling's *The Family Diamond. Simon Says... Marry Me!* is the premiere of Myrna Mackenzie's THE WEDDING AUCTION. Don't miss a single story in this engaging three-book miniseries. A pregnant bride-for-hire dreams of making *The Double Heart Ranch* a real home, but first she must convince her husband in this heart-tugger by Leanna Wilson. And *If the Ring Fits...* some lucky woman gets to marry a prince! In this sparkling debut Romance from Melissa McClone, an accident-prone American heiress finds herself a royal bride-to-be!

In coming months, look for Diana Palmer, a Joan Hohl-Kasey Michaels duet and much more. It's an exciting year for Silhouette Books, and we invite you to join the celebration!

Happy Reading!

*Mary-Theresa Hussey*

Mary-Theresa Hussey
Senior Editor

Please address questions and book requests to:
Silhouette Reader Service
U.S.: 3010 Walden Ave., P.O. Box 1325, Buffalo, NY 14269
Canadian: P.O. Box 609, Fort Erie, Ont. L2A 5X3

# THE FAMILY DIAMOND

## Moyra Tarling

R O M A N C E™
Published by Silhouette Books
America's Publisher of Contemporary Romance

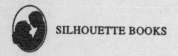

**SILHOUETTE BOOKS**

ISBN 0-373-19428-5

THE FAMILY DIAMOND

Copyright © 2000 by Moyra Tarling

**Books by Moyra Tarling**

---

## MOYRA TARLING

was born in Aberdeenshire, Scotland. It was there that she was first introduced to and became hooked on romance novels. In 1968, she immigrated to Vancouver, Canada, where she met and married her husband. They have two grown children. Empty-nesters now, they enjoy taking trips in their getaway van and browsing in antique shops for corkscrews and buttonhooks. But Moyra's favorite pastime is curling up with a great book—a romance, of course! Moyra loves to hear from readers. You can write to her at P.O. Box 161, Blaine, WA 98231-0161.

# IT'S OUR 20th ANNIVERSARY!
## We'll be celebrating all year,
## continuing with these fabulous titles,
## on sale in February 2000.

### Special Edition

 **#1303 Man...Mercenary...Monarch**
Joan Elliott Pickart

 **#1304 Dr. Mom and the Millionaire**
Christine Flynn

 **#1305 Who's That Baby?**
Diana Whitney

**#1306 Cattleman's Courtship**
Lois Faye Dyer

 **#1307 The Marriage Basket**
Sharon De Vita

 **#1308 Falling for an Older Man**
Trisha Alexander

### Intimate Moments

 **#985 The Wildes of Wyoming—Chance**
Ruth Langan

 **#986 Wild Ways**
Naomi Horton

 **#987 Mistaken Identity**
Merline Lovelace

**#988 Family on the Run**
Margaret Watson

 **#989 On Dangerous Ground**
Maggie Price

**#990 Catch Me If You Can**
Nina Bruhns

### Romance

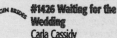 **#1426 Waiting for the Wedding**
Carla Cassidy

 **#1427 Bringing Up Babies**
Susan Meier

**#1428 The Family Diamond**
Moyra Tarling

 **#1429 Simon Says...Marry Me!**
Myrna Mackenzie

**#1430 The Double Heart Ranch**
Leanna Wilson

**#1431 If the Ring Fits...**
Melissa McClone

### Desire

**#1273 A Bride for Jackson Powers**
Dixie Browning

 **#1274 Sheikh's Temptation**
Alexandra Sellers

**#1275 The Daddy Salute**
Maureen Child

**#1276 Husband for Keeps**
Kate Little

**#1277 The Magnificent M.D.**
Carol Grace

**#1278 Jesse Hawk: Brave Father**
Sheri WhiteFeather

# *Chapter One*

Maura O'Sullivan stood at the foot of the wooden stairs leading up to the veranda of the elegant two-storied ranch house.

The taxi had pulled away. There was no turning back. Suddenly, a feeling of apprehension and excitement scampered along her nerve-endings, and the courage and conviction that had brought her to California in search of the father she'd believed was dead, seemed to drain out of her.

The urge to call out to the taxi driver, to tell him she'd made a mistake almost overwhelmed her....

"I thought I heard a car pull up." At the sound of the deep masculine voice Maura felt her pulse take a crazy leap. She quickly corralled her misgivings and glanced up at the man who'd appeared on the veranda from the side of the house.

Dressed in faded blue jeans and a white T-shirt,

Spencer Diamond was even more handsome than she remembered. Oozing confidence, and with a hint of arrogance in his step, he came down the stairs to meet her.

"Welcome to California!" He stopped in front of her.

"Thank you," she replied as she met his steady blue gaze.

"Why didn't you call from the bus station? I could have driven the wagon into town and picked you up," Spencer said as he picked up the suitcase and bag at her feet.

"I don't suppose you mean one of those old covered wagons, do you?" Maura asked, interest and humor lacing her tone.

Spencer held her gaze for a fleeting moment and instantly felt that sharp tug of attraction he'd experienced the first time he set eyes on Maura O'Sullivan two months ago in Kentucky.

He smiled and shook his head. "Afraid not. Covered wagons are only permitted on the roads during Kincade's annual Easter Parade or on special occasions such as weddings."

"Oh...I see." Disappointment echoed through her voice. "Ever since I was a little girl I've always wanted a ride in a real covered wagon, like the ones the settlers used when they made the trip across the country to California."

"One of my father's friends collects pioneer memorabilia," Spencer told her. "Perhaps while you're here I can arrange a tour for you, and maybe even a ride in one of the wagons."

"That would be lovely," Maura responded warmly.

"How was your bus trip?" Spencer asked as they climbed the stairs.

"Better than a wagon ride I guess," she joked. "But long and tiring just the same."

Spencer ushered her ahead of him, giving him the opportunity to study her. She wore a jean jacket and coffee-colored shirt and a pair of jeans that fit snugly, accentuating the rounded curve of her bottom.

A mass of coppery-red hair cascaded down her back in riotous disarray and framed a heart-shaped face he'd never quite been able to forget.

Not for the first time Spencer wondered at the reason for Maura's complete change of heart. Two months ago, while he and his parents had been visiting a stud farm near Lexington, Kentucky, he'd happened to mention to a group of his host's friends the difficulties he was having with one of his prize racehorses.

One of the guests proceeded to tell him about Maura O'Sullivan, a local horse trainer, extolling her talents and the almost magical success she'd had working with troubled and abused horses.

Spencer had voiced his skepticism, but his host had assured him Maura O'Sullivan could indeed work magic.

Later that same evening he'd come face-to-face with the stunning redhead and, deciding he had nothing to lose and everything to gain, he'd told her about Indigo and invited her to his ranch in California.

He recalled quite vividly the scornful look she'd subjected him to, before none-too-politely tossing his invitation back in his face, repeating a few of the negative comments she'd undoubtedly overheard him make.

That's why her call a week ago asking if he still needed help with his horse had come as something of a shock. But with little progress being made with Indigo, and an important race less than ten days away, he'd been hard-pressed to turn down her offer.

"You have a beautiful home," Maura commented.

"Thank you. The stables are out back. I'll give you a tour later," Spencer said.

As they approached the front door it was suddenly opened and Maura instantly recognized the attractive, silver-haired woman smiling at her.

"Maura! I thought I heard voices. It's so good to see you." Nora Diamond's greeting was warm and sincere, and Maura suddenly found herself enveloped in a welcoming hug.

At the unexpected embrace tears stung her eyes and she quickly blinked them away. "Thank you, Mrs. Diamond. It's good to see you. You're looking well."

"Thank you," Nora replied, stepping aside. "Please, come in. How was your journey? Can I offer you a cup of coffee?"

"The trip was tiring, and thank you, I never say no to a cup of coffee," Maura replied.

"Spencer, dear, take Maura's suitcase up to her room."

"Of course, Mother." Spencer was already heading for the stairs.

Maura followed Nora across the tiled foyer and along a hallway past a large dining room and on into a bright, spacious kitchen.

A large wooden butcher block occupied the center of the room, and forming a U-shape around it, and all within easy access, was the stove, fridge and double sink.

The cupboards were painted a pristine white, and the countertop, in a contrasting slate blue, matched the large venetian tiles covering the floor.

The work area was well laid out and Maura especially liked the array of copper pots and pans hanging from the ceiling above the butcher block.

A round oak table and six matching chairs sat near a bay window that overlooked the veranda. Beyond that lay the garden, and in the distance Maura could see the rooftops of buildings and guessed they were the stables.

"What a beautiful kitchen," Maura commented.

"Thank you. Please have a seat," Nora invited as she crossed to the counter. "So tell me, how was your trip?"

"Very nice, thank you," Maura replied politely. "I love watching the changing countryside." She didn't drive and hated flying. The two-day bus trip across five states had been a pleasant alternative.

Throughout the journey she'd been preoccupied with trying to formulate a plan of how she could arrange a meeting with her father.

Maura had only learned of her father's existence a month ago. She'd been cleaning out a closet full of her mother's things when she'd come across an old shoebox. Inside she'd found a variety of papers including an old journal written in her mother's handwriting.

Intrigued, Maura had read the daily entries written by her mother at the age of twenty-one. But when Maura reached the entry describing in detail the warm summer day her mother met a handsome young man named Michael Carson, the tone and content of the journal changed dramatically.

They'd bumped into each other at the Bridlewood Country Fair, and from that day forward Bridget Murphy's journal had been filled with the romantic musings of a young woman in love.

Maura soon realized that her mother and the young man had become lovers. But a month after their first meeting, Mickey, as her mother had affectionately called him, had returned to California. After his departure the journal entries had begun to dwindle until they stopped altogether.

Maura couldn't help feeling disappointed that the romance hadn't worked out. About to close the journal she'd noticed an envelope tucked between its worn pages.

The envelope written in her mother's handwriting was addressed to Michael Carson, Walnut Grove, Kincade, California. The letter had been opened and read, but scrawled across the address were the words Return to Sender.

Inside was a letter her mother had written. It began:

"Dear Mickey...I'm going to have a baby, your baby..."

Stunned, she'd read the journal and letter again, noting the date on the letter was two months before she was born. Michael Carson was her father.

At first she hadn't known what to do or where to turn. But after making a few discreet phone calls she'd discovered that Michael Carson still resided in the small California town of Kincade.

"What do you take in your coffee?" The question came from Spencer as he crossed to the table, carrying a tray with cups and saucers, cream and sugar. She'd been too distracted by her thoughts to hear his return, but his deep, resonant voice quickly brought her attention to the present.

Maura met Spencer's blue gaze, and for several long seconds she knew exactly how a deer felt when it found itself trapped in the glare of headlights.

Her breath snagged in her throat, and a guilty warmth crept up her neck and over her face. Her heart reacted, too, knocking wildly against her ribs.

"Uh...sorry." she muttered. "I was daydreaming,

enjoying the view," she said, flashing a nervous smile.

"Really," Spencer commented. "From the way you were frowning, I'd bet my bottom dollar you were puzzling over something. A problem perhaps?" He held her gaze, almost as if he was trying to see inside her head. "Am I right?"

Maura swallowed to alleviate the sudden dryness in her throat. He was too perceptive, by far. And the fact that he had reservations about her was easy to see.

In truth she couldn't really blame him. She'd been deliberately and unpardonably rude two months ago when she'd turned down his initial invitation to his ranch, but his arrogant behavior and skeptical comments had rubbed her the wrong way and she'd seen no reason to accept.

Her call asking if he still needed her help was a complete about-face, and she'd known as she talked to him she was the last person he'd expected to hear from.

The real reason she'd made the call was she'd remembered that the Blue Diamond Ranch was located in Kincade, California, the same town as the address on the letter she'd found in her mother's journal.

"There's that frown again," Spencer teased, but Maura heard the slight edge to his voice.

"Spencer, dear, behave," his mother admonished as she brought the coffee carafe and a plate of cookies to the table. "Maura's probably weary from the long bus ride."

Maura flashed Spencer's mother a grateful smile. "The coffee smells wonderful," she said.

"Cream and sugar?" Spencer asked politely, as his mother filled three cups, then returned to the counter to replace the carafe in the coffee machine.

"Cream, thank you," Maura replied, forcing herself to meet Spencer's blue gaze. The glint of humor together with the infectious grin slowly spreading across his handsome features caught her off guard and sent her pulse skittering wildly.

"You're welcome, red." He poured cream into her cup.

Maura bristled at the use of the detested nickname. She dropped her gaze, stifling the urge to tell him not to call her "red," knowing full well that to voice her displeasure would surely result in Spencer using the nickname at every possible opportunity just to annoy her.

Schooling her features, she glanced at him once more and for a dizzying moment Maura wondered if her heart had stopped beating. The air between them crackled with tension and something much more dangerous. Her heart restarted itself, beating at an irregular pace.

An emotion she couldn't define flared briefly in those dazzling blue eyes before it vanished, making her wonder if she'd seen it at all.

"I thought your father would be back by now," Nora commented as she rejoined them at the table.

"Where is Dad?" Spencer asked, leaning back casually in his chair.

"He had a few errands to run," his mother replied. "He said he'd be back by four, but it's nearly five. Oh...here he is now," she added as the kitchen door opened and her husband appeared.

"Sorry I'm late, dear." Elliot Diamond dropped a kiss on the top of his wife's head. He smiled at Maura. "Hi, Maura. It's nice to see you again. Did you have a good trip?"

"Yes, thank you," Maura replied politely.

"Why are you late?" Nora asked her husband.

"Oh...I stopped by Michael's place on my way home. I picked up a few groceries and put them in his fridge. He gets back from his cruise tomorrow, remember?"

"Of course!" Nora said. "Was everything all right over there?"

"Everything looked fine," Elliot assured his wife before turning to Maura. "We've had a rash of break-ins in the area recently and so we try to look out for each other. Michael Carson is a neighbor and one of our oldest and dearest friends. Is that fresh coffee I smell?" he asked, moving to the counter.

Maura felt the blood drain from her face and her heart slam against her breastbone at the mention of her father's name. Surely she'd heard wrong?

"Did you say your neighbor is Michael Carson?" Her voice seemed to come from somewhere far away.

"Yes," Elliot Diamond answered as he poured

himself a coffee. "He owns Walnut Grove, the adjoining property," he went on. "He and his wife had been our friends for more years than I care to remember. He's a widower now and has been for over a year. Do you know him?"

# Chapter Two

Maura couldn't breathe. Her chest felt tight, and she wondered for a moment if she was having a heart attack. To learn that her father was a close friend of the Diamond family was a bonus she hadn't expected.

Realizing everyone was staring at her, waiting for her to respond, she gathered her scattered thoughts and with a calmness she was far from feeling forced air into her lungs.

"I'm sorry. It's Mitchell, not Michael, who I was thinking of. Mitchell Carson was an old friend of my mother's," she quickly improvised, hoping she didn't sound too foolish. "I haven't seen him in years." She smiled. "Your neighbor was on a cruise, you say? That must be a wonderful way to spend a holiday.

"I've never been on a boat or a ship. Well, that's

not strictly true," she hurried on nervously. "I have ridden in a motorboat, but a cruise ship…that's totally different." She paused briefly for breath.

"I read somewhere that the cruise ships they're building these days are as tall as some skyscrapers," she soldiered on. She knew she was babbling but she couldn't seem to stop. "Have you and Elliot been on a cruise?" she asked.

"As a matter of fact we've been on several," Nora Diamond replied.

"Oh…where did you cruise to?" Maura asked, relieved that she appeared to have succeeded in smoothing over those awkward moments.

Though she longed to find out more about their neighbor, Michael Carson, the man who was her father, she decided it would be best to steer clear of the subject, at least for now.

Nora turned to her husband. "Our first cruise was to Alaska, wasn't it dear?"

For the next few minutes Maura heard about their cruise experiences, and though she listened attentively and asked questions, beneath her outward show of interest her thoughts were in turmoil.

To add to her agitation she was intensely aware of Spencer's penetrating gaze. He'd risen from the table and was leaning against the counter giving the impression of a casual listener, but there was nothing casual in the way his blue gaze remained focused on her.

She had the distinct impression he hadn't been taken in at all by her stumbling attempts to redirect the conversation, or her interest in cruising. And the frown that darkened his handsome features confirmed he was still puzzling over her reaction.

Maura brought her hand to her mouth to stifle a yawn.

Her hostess was quick to notice. "Maura, my dear, you must be exhausted, and I'm chattering on about cruises."

"I'm sorry," Maura said. "I guess the bus ride made me more tired than I thought."

"Spencer, show Maura to her room," Nora continued. "You can relax for a while. Have a nap. Dinner is at seven."

Maura rose from the chair. "Thanks for coffee."

Spencer eased himself away from the counter. "If you'd like to come this way."

Maura kept her smile in place and followed Spencer from the kitchen. He was silent as he led her up the oak stairs.

"The house is beautiful," Maura commented. "Have you lived here all your life?"

"Yes," Spencer said. "The Blue Diamond Ranch has been in our family for several generations."

"Are all the neighboring properties horse ranches, too?" she asked.

"No," he responded, but he didn't elaborate on his answer as she'd hoped. The temptation to ask him about Walnut Grove was strong, but she kept silent. At the top of the stairs Spencer turned left. Halfway down the corridor he came to a halt.

"Your bedroom has its own bathroom," he told her as he opened the door.

"Thank you." Maura started to cross the threshold, but Spencer's hand came out to stop her. "Do you know Michael Carson?" he asked abruptly.

Maura heard the hint of tension in his voice, and, careful to keep her expression neutral, she met his gaze.

"No, I've never had the pleasure," she replied truthfully, ignoring the prickle of sensation darting up her arm caused, she knew, by his fingers resting on the sleeve of her jean jacket.

Spencer held her gaze for what seemed an eternity. He was searching her face for...what? She didn't know. Her heart sounded like a drum-roll crescendo in her ears, and he was standing so close she was sure he must hear it.

"I'll see you at dinner," he said before turning and striding away.

Maura stepped inside the carpeted room and closed the door. She leaned against it for support and, taking several deep breaths, waited for her heart to slow to a more normal pace.

Her thoughts turned to her father and the fact that she might not have to wait too long to meet him. If Michael Carson was a close a friend of the Diamond family, it was possible he'd drop in for a neighborly visit.

Maura's breath hitched and her pulse gathered speed at the prospect of meeting her father, the man she hadn't known existed until a month ago.

She wasn't surprised to learn that he'd been married. But the fact that he was now a widower simplified matters a little. Her trip to California had been impulsive, but she had no intention of creating any kind of problem for him.

Restless, she crossed to the stylish French doors leading onto a small balcony. Opening the doors she stepped outside.

The sun had already gone down, but a faint trail of pink tinged the darkening sky along with a smattering of stars. The air had cooled, and a breeze tugged at her hair. She sighed, welcoming the caress that helped calm the jittery excitement inside her.

Not for the first time she wished there had been a photograph of Michael Carson amongst her mother's personal things, but other than the journal and the letter there had been nothing.

She would have to be patient. It was fortunate that he was returning from, rather than setting out on, his cruise.

Her mother's death a year ago from cancer had left Maura without family—no brothers, sisters, aunts, uncles, cousins or grandparents. Though her mother had married Brian O'Sullivan when Maura was three, they'd never had children of their own.

Maura had often wondered why her mother had married Brian, who, at her mother's insistence, had legally adopted Maura. But her childhood dream of being part of a real family, of having a father who loved her unconditionally had been quickly crushed.

In Brian O'Sullivan's eyes she was another man's

child, and for the most part he ignored her. His bouts of drinking turned him into a mean and angry man, and Maura soon learned to stay out of his way.

The marriage lasted three years, dissolving after her mother finally tired of her stepfather's constant drinking and verbal abuse. For Maura it was a relief to be rid of him, but his negative presence had only heightened her longing for her real father.

She'd tried asking her mother questions about him, only to be told the subject was off-limits. Though she'd known her mother had loved her, Maura always had the impression that having a child out of wedlock had been something of a burden for her. And Maura had been envious of friends who were lucky enough to have a loving, caring father.

Learning that her own father was alive and living in California had rocked her to the core, and she knew she would never rest until she'd met him face-to-face and asked him why he'd turned his back on her and her mother all those years ago.

She needed to know. She deserved to know.

Reentering the bedroom, she noticed the tasteful decor. A cream-colored carpet covered the floor, and the bedroom furniture, made from mahogany, consisted of a dressing table with matching nightstands and a beautifully carved headboard on the queen-size bed.

The bedspread reminded Maura of a field of wildflowers, and the walls, painted a pale shade of apricot, gave the room a cool ambience.

Crossing to her suitcase she lifted it onto the bed and proceeded to unpack.

Spencer stood at the wet bar in the dining room and poured himself a generous serving of whisky. His parents were in the kitchen putting the finishing touches on the meal.

Ten years ago his father had handed the business of running the ranch over to Spencer. Since then his father derived a great deal of pleasure from puttering around in the kitchen.

During the years he and his brother and sister had been growing up, his mother had hired a cook. And once they'd all left home for college or a career, his mother hadn't had the heart to let Mrs. B. go. Mrs. B. had taught her new and apt pupil, Elliot Diamond, everything she knew, while his mother had happily encouraged her husband to take over in the kitchen.

Spencer smiled. After more than forty years of marriage his parents were still very much in love and truly enjoyed each other's company. And when Spencer had married Lucy, he'd been sure that theirs would be the kind of marriage that would last.

He'd been wrong. His marriage had been nothing short of a disaster, souring his dreams and leaving him adrift on a sea of pain and bitterness.

A faint sound caught his attention, and he turned to see Maura standing in the doorway dressed in a cream blouse and rainbow-colored skirt that reached her ankles. Her coppery hair was tamed into a severe knot at the base of her elegant neck.

"Come in," he invited, aware once more of a swift jab of attraction at the sight of her. "May I pour you a drink?" he asked, deciding he liked her much better with her hair flowing free, the way he'd seen her the first time they met. He was sorely tempted to walk over and remove the pins.

"Soda water would be nice, thank you," she replied. She came toward him, stopping on the other side of the bar.

"Are you sure I can't interest you in a glass of Chardonnay? Or a Riesling perhaps? California wineries produce some of the best wines in the world."

She nibbled thoughtfully on her lower lip, and instantly his stomach muscles clenched and an emotion, long dormant, stirred deep inside him.

"Thank you. I'd love to try a California Chardonnay."

"Good choice," he replied. Setting his glass on the bar, he opened the small fridge below the counter and brought out a bottle of wine.

With practiced ease he stripped off its foil cover and withdrew the cork with the aid of a big brass corkscrew clamped onto the bar.

"Now there's a clever device," Maura commented. She watched him pour the pale gold liquid into a wineglass.

"And very efficient," he said, handing her the glass.

"Thank you." Her fingers brushed his and at the

fleeting contact, a shiver of sensation darted up her arm. She threw him a startled glance, and as their gazes collided, her heart lurched painfully and her breath froze in her throat.

"There you are, Maura," Nora Diamond's greeting shattered the tension-filled silence. It was with some relief Maura turned to her hostess. "Is your room comfortable?" Nora asked.

"It's lovely, thank you," Maura responded.

"Be sure and let me know if you need anything," Nora said with a smile. "Is that Chardonnay you're drinking?"

Maura nodded. "Your son kindly poured me a glass."

"Spencer, dear. I'll have one, too," his mother said. "Oh...and, Maura, when it comes to mealtimes, they're usually a casual affair. My husband told me to announce that dinner's ready, so please take a seat anywhere at the table," she went on. "If you'll excuse me, I'll go and give Elliot a hand."

Careful to avoid Spencer's gaze, Maura crossed to the oak dining table. Setting down her glass she pulled out the nearest chair.

"How's the wine?" Spencer asked coming up behind her. He held the chair for her, and as she sat down she could feel his warm breath fanning the back of her neck.

Awareness danced across her skin, leaving a trail of heat in its wake. It took every ounce of control to stop her hand from shaking as she reached for her wineglass.

She sipped the Chardonnay, more to steady her nerves than to taste, and as the silky coolness slide down her throat, the tension inside her slowly began to ease.

"Hmm....it's lovely. Refreshing, with a crisp fruity taste," she said brightly.

"I'm impressed." Spencer placed the glass his mother had ordered next to a place setting. "And here I thought folks from Kentucky only drank bourbon."

"Oh...we do." Maura heard the humor in his voice and fought to hide a grin. "And it's the best bourbon in the world, as you know. But there are some of us who have actually been known to recognize a decent glass of wine when we taste one."

Spencer emitted a low rumble of laughter. The sound sent a fresh flurry of sensation chasing down her spine.

Suddenly Elliot appeared carrying a steaming platter to the table. He flashed Maura a smile as he set down a dish of chicken breasts drowning in a creamy mushroom sauce.

Nora followed with two serving dishes, one containing steamed potatoes, the other a variety of vegetables.

Once they were seated and the food served, conversation drifted easily from one subject to another as they ate.

Spencer occupied the chair directly across from Maura, and she found it both annoying and disconcerting that each time their gazes met her heart skipped a beat.

"Did you say Michael is due home tomorrow?" The question came from Spencer, and Maura quickly shook off the feeling of fatigue slowly descending on her and, holding her breath, waited for a response.

"I believe he gets in sometime in the afternoon," Nora reported.

"Where exactly was he cruising to?" Maura asked hoping to keep the subject of her father in the forefront.

"The Caribbean," Elliot replied. "Though I don't recall which ports of call he was visiting."

"Does he travel a lot?" Maura asked, her tone light.

"Yes. He and his wife enjoyed taking trips," Nora answered. "We went on several vacations with them when Ruth was alive. This is the first trip he's taken since her death."

"He must still miss his wife," Maura said, cautiously careful not to sound too interested.

"Very much," Elliot replied.

"I'm afraid Michael's had more than his share of sorrow these past few years," Nora added, darting a concerned glance at her son.

Puzzled, Maura looked across the table at Spencer.

"Michael also lost his daughter, Lucy, who happened to be my wife," Spencer said. His tone was level, his voice carefully controlled.

Maura fought not to react, but inside she was reeling. From the brief conversation earlier she'd learned her father had been married, but somehow the knowledge that he'd had another daughter, that she'd had a half sister—and that her half sister had been married to Spencer—was something of a shock.

"Lucy was an only child." Nora picked up the thread, effectively capturing Maura's attention. "She and Spencer had only been married a year..." Nora came to a halt, glancing once more at her son before continuing. "Lucy died in a car accident two years ago. Ruth never really recovered from her daughter's death."

Maura drew a steadying breath and met Spencer's gaze. His eyes were shuttered, his expression unreadable. It was obvious that the pain of losing his wife still lingered, and her heart went out to him.

"How tragic. I'm so sorry for your loss," Maura said.

Spencer looked away, making no reply. He reached for his water glass.

"Lucy was a beautiful young woman," Elliot commented, filling the silence and drawing Maura away from Spencer. "Being an only child she was spoiled and a little reckless."

"Lucy's death hit us all very hard," Nora went on. She threw her son a compassionate glance. "Ruth simply never got over it, dying a year later of a broken heart."

"Difficult as it's been for Michael, we saw this

trip as a sign he's starting to come to terms with the tragedy and moving on with his life,'' Elliot said.

As Maura listened to Nora and Elliot talk about their daughter-in-law, she was both puzzled and intrigued by Spencer's silence. He appeared to have withdrawn to some private place.

Nora rose from the table, and started to gather up the dishes, bringing an end to the conversation.

"Let me help," Maura said.

"You'll do no such thing, at least not tonight," Nora asserted good-naturedly. "Stay and chat with Spencer."

Maura's heart skipped a beat. She would have preferred to follow her hostess and talk more about Michael Carson.

"Coffee anyone?" Elliot asked, reappearing with carafe in hand.

"I'll have coffee, Dad." Spencer pushed back his chair and crossed to the bar.

"Yes, thank you," Maura replied. "And the chicken was delicious. My compliments to the chef."

"Thank you," Elliot responded as he began to pour coffee into cups.

"Maura? Can I interest you in a liqueur? There's Brandy? Cointreau? Or how about Grand Marnier?" Spencer offered.

"No, thank you," Maura replied. She stood up. "Actually I think I'll pass on the coffee. It's been a long day, I'm rather tired. I'll just say good-night."

"By all means, my dear," Elliot said.

Maura dropped her napkin on the table and made her way from the room. She stopped for a moment in the doorway and glanced at Spencer, who was pouring himself a liqueur. She could see the tension in his shoulders and in the line of his jaw, almost as if he was gritting his teeth.

The conversation at dinner had obviously upset him more than he was willing to show. Ever since Lucy's name had been mentioned, she'd noticed his withdrawal and noticed, too, that the atmosphere in the room had changed from lighthearted to melancholy.

Even now he appeared to be deep in thought, and Maura could only guess that the loss of his wife was still a raw and painful wound.

He must have loved Lucy very much. Turning, Maura headed for the stairs, feeling a stab of envy for Lucy, the sister she'd never known.

Maura lay awake for some time, thinking about Spencer's wife, Lucy. The possibility of having a sibling had crossed her mind, but finding out she'd had a half sister who was now gone left her torn between feelings of joy and a deep regret that she would forever be denied the opportunity to know her.

She tried to imagine what it had been like for Lucy growing up with their father. From the little she'd gleaned from the conversation at dinner, Lucy's parents had spoiled her.

Maura felt tears slowly trickle into her hair. It

seemed so unfair. Being part of a family was all she'd ever wanted. Growing up without a father, she'd often been made to feel like an outsider.

And even now that she'd located him, there was no guarantee he'd welcome her with open arms or want to have anything to do with her. He'd *had* a daughter, a daughter he'd loved and lost.

Michael Carson had turned his back on Maura and her mother twenty-seven years ago. He could easily do it again.

It was with these thoughts swirling in her head that Maura finally drifted off to sleep. When she awoke, the room was in darkness and for a moment she couldn't remember where she was.

Rolling onto her back, she stretched. A glance at the digital clock on the bedside table told her it was 4:55. She lay for several minutes enjoying the warmth and comfort of the queen-size bed.

Pushing the covers aside, she rose and went to the sliding doors. Outside on the balcony she inhaled deeply, taking in the familiar and much-loved scent of horses and hay and the outdoors.

The air was fresh and invigorating and not as chilly as it would have been had she been standing on her small front porch back in Bridlewood.

The sun was still abed but the faint glow to the east told her it would soon be making an appearance. Restless and suddenly eager to begin work with the horse she'd come to help, she decided to take a walk outside and locate the stables.

Slipping back into her room she indulged in a

quick shower before dressing in her jeans and pale-blue cotton shirt. She braided her still-wet hair into one long ponytail. Out of habit Maura made up her bed and, with her riding boots in her hand, headed downstairs.

When she reached the kitchen, she came to an abrupt halt at the sight of Spencer scooping ground coffee into the automatic coffeemaker.

For a moment she was tempted to sneak away, but she wasn't quick enough.

"Good morning. Coffee will be ready in a few minutes. Would you care to join me?"

"That would be lovely, thank you," Maura replied politely, noting, as she came farther into the kitchen, the weary slant of his shoulders and the lines around his eyes.

"I hope you slept well," said Spencer.

"Like a baby," Maura replied as she crossed to the table, annoyed at the nervous flutter of her stomach. "What about you?"

"I didn't sleep at all," he replied, tiredness seeping into his voice. He glanced up and met her gaze head-on. "I had a few things on my mind."

Maura felt her heart kick against her rib cage in alarm.

"Really," she said cautiously, unsure just how she should respond. "I don't suppose there's anything I can do, is there?" she asked out of politeness.

Spencer switched on the coffeemaker and turned to give her his full attention.

"Actually, there is," he said, his gaze hard and unyielding, sending a quiver of alarm racing through her. "Perhaps you can explain to me why, after turning down my invitation two months ago to come to California, you suddenly called to say you'd changed your mind?"

# Chapter Three

Spencer studied Maura's startled expression with interest. Ever since her strange and unforgettable reaction to hearing Michael Carson's name, he'd become both wary and suspicious.

Her nervous chatter, followed by her comments on cruises, ships and holidays, had only added to his unease. For a fleeting moment she'd reminded him of Lucy, who'd been an expert at hiding the truth.

At dinner he'd deliberately brought up the subject of Michael Carson, just to see Maura's reaction. He'd caught the flash of keen interest in her hazel eyes, as well as the sudden tension in her body. She'd held her breath, just as she was doing now.

"Cat got your tongue, red?" Spencer asked and saw annoyance and guilt war with each other in the depths of her eyes.

"I felt bad, that's all," Maura replied, inwardly bristling at his use of the hated nickname.

"Really?" he said, his tone telling her he didn't for a minute believe her.

"I was rude to you that night. Afterward I regretted my outburst." She hoped she sounded convincing. "I realized that the best way to prove how wrong your assumptions were about me was to come to California and show you just what I can do. By turning you down that night I was really punishing the horse, not you."

Spencer laughed. The low throaty sound sent her pulse skyrocketing.

"That's very good," he said. "But that was two months ago. You took your time...thinking it over. Why did it take you so long to call?"

Maura glared at him. He had her over a barrel, but she wasn't about to give in without a fight. "Look...if you don't want my help with Indigo you should have said so when I called, that way we could have saved each other a lot of time and expense—"

Spencer heard the genuine indignation and anger in her voice, and for a moment he was tempted to believe her. In truth he wanted to believe that her only reason for coming to California was to work with his prize-winning racehorse, but he simply didn't buy it.

He remembered vividly their encounter that night two months ago. He'd have bet money on never hearing from her again. And while he acknowledged that he really had very little to back up his sense of unease, he wasn't a man who ignored his instincts, not anymore.

Silently he admired the spark of challenge and defiance he could see in her eyes. But if she wasn't hiding something, why was she chewing nervously on her lower lip?

Confrontation hadn't worked; perhaps he needed to try another approach. "I do need your help with Indigo," he replied, deciding to bide his time, to wait and watch. "Look...I'm sorry," he went on, and noted with some satisfaction the glint of relief that danced briefly in her eyes.

"That's all right." Maura brushed aside his apology and tried to ignore the way her heart flip-flopped crazily inside her chest.

His question, though not unexpected, had surprised her. But even more startling had been the fact that for a mind-numbing second, as the silence stretched between them, she'd been sorely tempted to confide in him, to tell him about her mother's journal and her startling discovery that Michael Carson was her father.

She'd quickly quashed the impulse. In all likelihood he wouldn't believe her. And she quickly reminded herself Spencer had been married to Lucy, Michael's daughter. His loyalty undoubtedly lay in that direction, and if she told him the truth, he'd accuse her of lying or something equally unpleasant and send her packing before she could meet her father.

If she stayed at the Diamond Ranch, her chances of coming face-to-face with Michael Carson were much higher. With that possibility in mind, she would concentrate on Indigo and pray that her father would pay his neighbors and friends a visit.

And if in the meantime she succeeded in helping Indigo overcome his problems, she might get the added bonus of earning Spencer's trust and respect.

"Do you still want coffee?" Spencer's question cut into her wandering thoughts.

"Yes. Thank you." Maura approached the counter. "Tell me more about Indigo."

Spencer retrieved two mugs from the cupboard above the sink and filled them. He slid one mug across the counter toward her, followed by the cream jug, then leaned against the butcher block, coffee in hand.

"I bought Indigo two years ago at a sale here in the California. Since then he's won all six races we've entered him in.

"Unfortunately, he's got a thing about starting gates, and with each race he's gotten progressively worse. At the last race two months ago the stewards came close to disqualifying him. He held up the proceedings for more than twenty minutes before they finally got him into the gate."

"Does he react the same way when he's being loaded into the horse van?" Maura asked.

"No. Well, at least not to the same degree," Spencer replied. "He balks at first but after a few tries we get him loaded. Why?"

"Just curious," she said. "When did you say he was due to race?"

"A week Saturday, at Santa Anita," Spencer answered. "And if he refuses to enter the starting gate, disrupts or delays the race in any way, he'll be disqualified and possibly banned from racing for life."

Maura heard the frustration and the echo of defeat in Spencer's voice. But she was encouraged by the fact that Indigo had been winning races even after wasting effort and energy refusing to go into the starting gate. He was obviously a gifted racer and it would be a sad day for both horse and owner if he were permanently banned from the sport.

"We don't have much time," Maura said. "When can I see him?" she asked, wanting not only to prove herself but also to ease the anxiety she could see on Spencer's rugged features. "I need to get to know him and gain his trust," she went on. "Once that's accomplished, I should be able to figure out what's causing him to fight the gate each time. Understanding the root of the problem often leads to a solution."

"I sincerely hope so," Spencer commented on a sigh. "Why don't we head down to the stables right now?"

"I'm ready." Maura set her near-empty mug on the counter. "I assume you have a daily schedule for all your horses. Does Indigo ride out with the rest of your string?" she asked.

"Yes," Spencer replied. "I thought it best not to deviate from his normal training schedule."

"Good." Maura retrieved her boots. "What exactly have you tried so far?" She sat down and pulled them on.

"Everything from putting a blindfold on him to bribing him with food. If anything, he's getting worse," Spencer added in a discouraging tone.

Maura stood up. "Let's check him out."

Indigo was truly a magnificent animal. There was no other way to describe the chestnut Thoroughbred with the distinguishing white blaze on his nose, standing quietly in his stall.

Spencer introduced Maura to the stable hand assigned to take care of the prize-winning racehorse. Joe was preparing to give Indigo his morning rub down.

"Did Phil say anything about his ride this morning?" Spencer asked.

"Just that Indy was raring to go, as always," Joe responded. "He sure loves to race. Phil says he has a hard time keeping Indy from going flat-out in the practice runs. He's pretty sure Indy will win the Jane Vanderhoof Cup for four-year-olds, no problem at all."

"Indigo will only win if we can get him to walk into that starting gate without breaking stride," Spencer commented. "When will you be finished here, Joe?"

"Give me half an hour," Joe replied as he prepared to enter Indigo's stall. Inside Indigo snorted softly in greeting.

Spencer turned to Maura. "Why don't I take you on a tour of the place? We'll come back when he's finished."

Maura had seen her share of racing stables, but never one quite so well run as the Blue Diamond Ranch. Spencer ran a tight ship and, judging by the nods and greetings he gave and received from the stable hands and riders they encountered, he was also well respected by the men who worked for him.

She met Hank Wilson, the stable manager, and toured the open-air and immaculately kept stables that housed a total of twenty racehorses. Of those, Spencer and his father owned part interest in two and full interest in one, Indigo.

Spencer also showed her the stable where the family's horses were kept, horses that were ridden mostly for pleasure, inviting her to take one out whenever she wanted, with the exception of his own mount, Lucifer.

As they made their way back to Indigo's stall, Maura asked, "Would you be offended if I asked you not to stay? I'd prefer to get to know him in my own way and in my own time."

In actual fact she didn't relish the thought of having Spencer standing nearby watching her every move. She found his presence and proximity more than a little unnerving, and knew Indigo would readily pick up on her reaction.

She caught the look of indecision that flitted across his tanned face.

"Yes, I'd be offended," Spencer began. "But I—"

"It's just that I know you don't wholeheartedly believe I'll be able to do anything," she cut in. "That translates to negative energy, and it's been my experience that horses of Indigo's caliber are usually highly sensitive creatures. He's bound to pick up on that negativity."

Spencer's mouth curved into a smile. "You didn't let me finish. You're right I'm skeptical, but that's because the stories I've heard about you make you out to be some kind of magician, a horse whisperer if you will."

Maura opened her mouth to protest, but he raised a hand to stop her.

"The truth is, my back is against the wall. I'm running out of time and options, and I have nothing to lose and everything to gain by giving you a free hand. I'll leave you to weave your…magic," he said. "No offense intended," he added with a grin.

A tingle of awareness shimmied through her, and Maura wondered if Spencer knew how potent was his smile.

"Thank you. I appreciate your honesty," she said. "I'm sure any story you heard has been embellished in the telling. But I'll be honest, too. While my methods might work with some horses, I've had my share of failures.

"Every situation has its challenges, every animal is unique," Maura went on. "I can't guarantee I'll be able to find that…ah…magical solution for Indigo, but the sooner I get started the better.''

''Fine. I'll leave you to it.'' With a nod he turned and strode away.

Maura drew a steadying breath and turned her attention to Indigo. She opened the door of his stall and stood studying his large frame, noting with admiration his clean lines and classic bone structure.

Aware of her presence, Indigo turned his head to stare at her. One look into his eyes confirmed he was a highly intelligent animal. His natural curiosity brought him over to where she stood, and when she extended her hand, palm up, he blew on it before turning to munch on the hay in the feed basket hanging nearby.

''You are a handsome fellow and no mistake,'' Maura told him, keeping her voice low. She moved inside the stall and was pleased when Indigo's only reaction was to throw her a cursory glance and continue eating.

Maura approached him and stroked his neck, allowing him to get accustomed to her presence. After a few minutes she placed both hands on his muscled shoulder and slowly began to move down his body toward his rear, noting as she did that he pressed against her hands and away from the wall of the stall.

Maintaining the pressure, she pushed against him and felt his muscles ripple seconds before his left hind foot kicked out. Maura immediately removed her hands and stepped back. Talking softly to him, she began stroking his neck once more.

She was encouraged by the fact that neither her presence nor her actions had caused him great concern. She proceeded to conduct a few more small tests, wanting to eliminate the possibility that he was being or had been abused.

His reactions to several threatening movements gave no such indication, but when she tried a second time to push him against the wall of his stall, he became restless and agitated, a sign she immediately connected with mild claustrophobia.

She stayed for another half hour settling him down and getting him accustomed to her voice, her touch and her scent. Exiting the stall, she wandered around on her own.

At the far end of the row of horse stalls she caught sight of Spencer talking to one of the men. Not wanting to intrude, she retraced her steps and made her way through the security gates and on up the path leading to the house.

The sun had begun its steady climb into a blue sky, and the temperature was already in the sixties. On reentering the kitchen, Maura was instantly assailed with the tantalizing smell of freshly baked muffins.

"Good morning!" The greeting came from Elliot Diamond, who stood at the sink. "Help yourself to coffee," he offered. "And there are bran muffins on the table. Did Spencer give you the grand tour?"

"Yes, he did," Maura replied. "You have a wonderful facility here," she said as she poured herself a cup of coffee.

"Thank you. Spencer deserves all the credit," his father said proudly. "Ever since he took over from me ten years ago he's put his heart and soul into the business and made it what it is today. But if you want my honest opinion, he spends far too much time working and rarely takes a break.

"His mother and I had hoped his marriage to Lucy would change all that, and I suppose for a while it did…" Elliot stopped. He turned his attention to the sink, almost as if he regretted his words.

"He must have been devastated when his wife died," Maura commented, hoping Elliot would continue to talk about his son. Instead he changed the subject.

"I suppose you met the pride of our stable?"

"If you mean Indigo, yes. And he's magnificent," Maura replied, her tone sincere. "I hope I can find a way to change his behavior."

"I wish you luck," Elliot said dryly. "We've tried everything. Much as I hate to say it, I think he's a lost cause. I doubt he'll race again."

"My father the optimist." The comment came from Spencer who'd appeared at the back door.

"Sorry, Son," Elliot said looking suitably repentant. "But you have to admit, what you need is a miracle."

"Dad, you probably don't realize it, but you've just insulted our guest." Humor laced his voice. "I did that in Kentucky, to my cost, I might add." He flashed a dazzling smile.

"Maura has come all this way to try to help us out," Spencer continued. "Don't you think we should give her our support? Besides, miracles do happen. And we've invested too much money in Indigo to write him off just yet."

"You're right," Elliot was quick to reply. He turned to Maura. "I hope you'll accept my apology. My comment wasn't directed at you personally or meant as a criticism."

"No offense taken," she assured him with a smile.

"If you'll excuse me," Elliot went on. "I promised my wife I'd take her into town this morning. Maura, please make yourself at home. We find that works best around here. I'll see you both later." With a wave he was gone.

Maura crossed to the table and reached for one of the muffins. Breaking off a piece she popped it into her mouth.

"So, tell me, how did you and Indigo get along?" Spencer asked as he helped himself to coffee.

"Fine," she replied. "He's well behaved and in beautiful condition."

"Any ideas on how you propose to tackle the problem?" he asked.

"I have several," she told him. "But first I have a few requests."

"Fire away."

"Do you have videos of his races?" she asked.

"I'm particularly interested in seeing what he's been doing at the starting gates. Oh, and I'm going to need a starting gate. Do you use one on your practice track?"

Spencer took a sip of coffee before answering.

"Videos I have," he said. "And yes, we have a starting gate on the practice track. Anything else?"

Maura broke off another piece of muffin. "Would it be possible for me to borrow Joe for a while, or Phil, if he's the one who regularly rides Indigo?

"I need someone who knows Indigo well to work with me on this. And do you have an enclosed area I can use, somewhere away from everything, where he won't easily be distracted. I want to put him through some basic schooling again, remind him of his manners."

"Sure… There's a covered ring on the north side of the stables," he said.

"I'll also need the use of a horse box, preferably the same one you use to transport him to and from the races. I want to see for myself how he behaves when he's being loaded in and taken out."

"I'll tell Hank to let you have anything you need," Spencer said. "When are you planning on getting started?"

"As soon as possible," Maura replied. "I'd like to look at the videos first."

"I'll pull them out for you," Spencer said. "But before you get down to work, and because it's such a beautiful spring day, I thought you might like to tour the rest of the Blue Diamond Ranch, but on horseback this time.''

Maura hesitated. Though she was anxious to start working with Indigo, the invitation to see the ranch was decidedly appealing. It appeared that Spencer was willing, for the time being, to set aside his reservations about her and her abilities. To refuse might jeopardize this tentative truce.

"Thanks, I'd like that," she said with a smile.

Spencer brought Lucifer to a halt beneath a stand of trees near the edge of a small lake. Maura, riding a sweet but spirited mare named Stardust, reined in beside him. The blue water of the lake sparkled like a diamond in the sunshine.

"This is a beautiful spot." She turned to Spencer and felt her heart careen against her ribs as her gaze lit on the man astride the big black horse.

The dark-brown Stetson he wore cast a shadow over his handsome face. He reminded Maura of a sheriff from an old Western movie. All that was missing was a shiny star to pin on the front of his denim shirt.

"It's one of my favorite places," he told her. "An oasis, you might say. My brother, Marsh, my sister, Piper, and I came here almost every day during the summer when we were kids. And every Sunday Mother would pack a picnic, and we'd all ride over to spend the afternoon cooling off under the shade of the trees or swimming in the lake.''

Spencer dismounted and tossed Lucifer's reins over a low bush.

Maura joined him on the ground and let the mare's reins fall, sure with Lucifer nearby she wouldn't wander off.

She followed Spencer into the shade of a weeping willow tree, silently envying him and his family and wishing she had memories of her own like the ones he'd mentioned.

"The water looks so inviting," Maura commented. "I bet you spent a lot of time swimming." The sun's rays winked at her off the water.

"You got that right," he replied. He removed his hat and wiped his forehead on the sleeve of his shirt. "And on a hot summer's night this is still the best place to skinny-dip. Have you ever gone skinny-dipping, Maura?" He flashed her a lopsided grin.

Maura's heart shuddered to a halt as an image of Spencer's long, lean, naked body, glistening in the moonlight as he walked out of the water, filled her mind.

She swallowed convulsively and felt her heart stumble before picking up its normal rhythm once more.

"No, I must admit, that's one experience I've missed." She kept her tone light, her gaze straight ahead.

"Believe me, there's nothing quite like it," Spencer said, his voice low and seductive.

"I'll take your word for it," Maura responded,

surprised by the strange heat slowly spreading through her.

"You know, I think it's warm enough for a dip," Spencer continued. "Want to give it a try?" The enticing invitation sent Maura's heart racing.

"I think not," she said a little shakily, already turning away. "But don't let me stop you...."

"Coward..." Spencer said, his voice barely a whisper.

Suddenly the air was rent with the sound of Stardust squealing.

Maura turned and instantly broke into a run when she saw the mare rear up, whinnying in fear and panic. Beside Stardust, Lucifer began to stamp and snort and nicker in alarm.

When Maura reached the horses she grabbed for Stardust's dangling reins, but the frightened animal tossed her head, then turned and raced away.

Lucifer was still shaking his head and pawing the ground as he tried to tug his reins free.

Maura turned to him. "Hey, boy, take it easy, it's all right." She took a step toward the skittish horse and reached out to grasp the bridle.

Lucifer had other ideas. Rearing up he began pawing the air dangerously close to Maura's face.

"Maura! Watch out!" Spencer shouted.

Maura wasn't altogether sure what happened next, but seconds later she was sprawling on her back on the dusty ground with Spencer on top of her.

Spencer slowly eased away from her, breathing hard.

"Are you completely and utterly mad?" He practically spat the words as he glared down at her. "You could have been killed."

"Don't be stupid," she retorted rudely. "I was perfectly fine until you ran me down," she told him, aware of his body pressed hard against hers and his warm breath fanning her face.

"Ran you down...!" He spluttered angrily. "Dammit, red! I just saved your life. Do you know how close those hooves came to that pretty little head of yours?"

"They weren't that close," she protested, refusing to acknowledge he was right. "What frightened them?" she asked. "And don't call me red," she added, annoyance ringing in her voice.

"It must have been a snake," Spencer replied. "That's the only thing that would set Lucifer off like that. And I'll call you red if I damn well feel like it."

Outraged, she opened her mouth to give him a piece of her mind, but whatever she'd been about to say was instantly forgotten when her gaze collided with his.

Tension arced between them like a breathing, living thing. She could feel Spencer's heart thundering in time with her own, and when his gaze shifted to her lips, her breath caught in her throat as every nerve in her body jolted to life.

When he slowly began to lower his mouth toward hers, her pulse went into overdrive.

"Don't you dare—" she began.

"Oh, I dare," Spencer said huskily. "You know, red, I've wanted to do this from the first moment I set eyes on you." With that he covered her mouth with his.

# Chapter Four

Maura's heart skidded to a halt the moment Spencer's lips claimed hers. His kiss was hot, wet, demanding. Desire spiraled through her with an intensity that frightened her.

She tried, with a quiet desperation, to hold on to her anger and indignation, use them as a protective shield against his sensual onslaught, but the pressure of Spencer's long, lean body pinning her to the ground from her breasts to her thighs was dangerously erotic, melting all thought of resistance.

His tongue teased, then entwined with hers in an erotic dance that left her breathless and aching. She'd never been kissed so thoroughly or so masterfully before, had never been made to feel this heady anticipation, this driving passion.

At twenty-seven Maura was still a virgin, but for the first time in her life, temptation, in the form of handsome and dynamic Spencer Diamond, was propelling her closer to the edge of reason.

She hadn't known desire could be so all consuming. She wanted him, with an urgency that shocked her to the core. This couldn't be happening! She hardly knew the man! She didn't even like him.

Appalled by her body's unprecedented reaction, Maura broke free of the kiss. She rolled away from Spencer and, taking several deep breaths, attempted to steady her racing heart.

Keeping her back to him, she hugged her knees, silently waiting for the need humming through her veins to subside.

Spencer sat up. "Well, well. That was very interesting," he said, feigning a nonchalance he was far from feeling. His heart pounded in his chest like a runaway horse, and the desire that had slammed into him with the force of a tornado hadn't even begun to recede.

He stood up, brushing dirt from his jeans, careful to avoid a certain sensitive part of his anatomy. A quick glance located his Stetson sitting a few feet away in the dirt. He retrieved it and used it as a screen to hide the tension lingering in his groin.

Maura swiped dust from her jeans as she rose. "It was just a kiss." She wanted to diminish the effect he'd had on her senses, but her voice wavered slightly, lessening the impact of her dismissal.

"That's not the impression I got," Spencer replied softly. She'd wanted him almost as much as he'd wanted her, and it was all he could do not haul her into his arms and prove she wasn't as unaffected as she pretended.

Maura met his gaze. "I wasn't out to impress," she told him with barely concealed annoyance. He held her gaze, amusement dancing in those dazzling blue eyes. Her face grew warm, and she could feel a blush slowly creep into her cheeks. She turned away.

"Stardust is gone," she said.

"She'll be halfway back to the stables by now," Spencer said. "Lucifer appears to have calmed down." He crossed to where the horse stood nearby.

Tugging free Lucifer's reins, Spencer swung into the saddle with an ease and grace that had Maura's pulse skipping a beat.

"Guess we'll have to ride double," Spencer said, nudging Lucifer toward her with his heels.

Maura's heart slammed against her ribs in response to his suggestion. "I can walk," she replied, determined to keep as much distance between them as possible.

Spencer's laughter only added to her irritation. "I know you can walk," he said. "Only it's a long way back to the stables. Lucifer can easily handle two riders. But if it's a problem for you..." His voice trailed off.

Maura heard the underlying challenge. She knew she was being foolish, but the effect of his kiss—a kiss she knew she'd never forget—still vibrated through her.

Shielding her eyes against the sun, she gazed up

at Spencer and for the second time in as many minutes felt her heart stumble. Oh, why did he have to be so handsome?

Though the brim of his Stetson shaded his eyes, she knew by the curve of his mouth that he was smiling at her.

He leaned toward her and held out his hand. Biting back a sigh, she swallowed her pride. Seconds later she was sitting behind him. Lucifer sidestepped a little, adjusting to the added weight, and in an action that was pure reflex Maura slid her arms around Spencer's waist to steady herself.

"All set?" he asked over his shoulder.

"Fine," Maura replied, though she was far from fine. The strong scent of male mingled with sunshine and earth and lemon and leather to send tiny shock waves of awareness across her nerve endings.

This fresh assault to her senses was almost more than she could handle. In an attempt to put some small margin of space between them, she leaned back a little, resting her hands on her thighs.

But when Lucifer started up the small incline leading away from the lake, Maura automatically leaned into Spencer, her breasts pressing against his back. For the second time in as many minutes her breath locked in her throat and her heart picked up speed.

Spencer was having problems of his own. The taste of Maura lingered in his mouth like a fine wine, and if that wasn't enough, he couldn't get the memory of her wild response out of his mind.

Added to that was the pressure of Maura's breasts against his back as Lucifer climbed up the trail leading away from the lake.

"I hope it's not too uncomfortable back there," he said, wanting to fill the silence and distract his own thoughts.

"I'm fine," she lied. "So, tell me about your family. I know you have a sister, Piper, and a brother, Marshall."

"Yes," Spencer replied. "Marshall is three years younger. He's a doctor. He came back to Kincade a year ago to take over as the new chief of staff at the hospital."

"Does he live in town?" she asked.

"Yes. He and his wife built a house over by the hospital. Kate's a nurse, but she's not working at the moment. She looks after Marsh's daughter, Sabrina, from his first marriage.

"Sabrina's going to have a brother or sister in another week or two," he added, and she heard a smile in his voice, revealing that the idea of a new niece or nephew pleased him immensely.

"How nice," Maura commented. "What about your sister?" she asked, wanting to find out more about his family.

"Piper is the baby of the family, she's a photographer and she lives in London...or at least she does when she's not gallivanting around Europe with her camera," Spencer explained.

Maura could tell by the warmth and affection in his voice that Spencer loved both siblings.

"Were you close growing up?" she probed.

"Marsh and I were pretty close," Spencer acknowledged. "Piper arrived on the scene much later. I was thirteen and Marsh ten. My mother jokingly refers to Piper as 'the afterthought.' By the time she came along, Marsh and I weren't too interested in babies."

Maura felt rather than heard the low rumble of laughter that followed his words. His memories of that time were obviously happy ones. Envy and an ache of longing tugged at her heart.

"My father insisted on Marsh and me learning how to feed and change her," he went on. "Neither of us thought much of that idea, but Dad argued that we were a family and as such we had to share responsibilities, including taking care of our new sister."

He was silent for a moment, and Maura smiled as she tried to conjure up an image of Spencer as a teenager, changing his sister's diaper.

"What did your mother think?" Maura asked, intrigued by the tale.

"She agreed wholeheartedly." He chuckled, then added, "Thankfully she let us off the hook when it came to night feedings."

They were both silent for a moment.

"When I think back on it," he continued, "we learned firsthand how much work there is to looking after a newborn baby. It certainly gave me a better understanding and appreciation of our parents. I think it brought us closer as a family, though I'm surprised Piper survived some of the rough handling she endured at Marsh's and my hands.

"She was one tough kid." He went on lovingly. "From the minute she could walk, she followed Marsh or me around like a puppy."

His voice trailed off, and Maura silently acknowledged that Nora and Elliot Diamond had done a great job raising their children. Spencer had obviously enjoyed a childhood filled with love, and not for the first time Maura felt a stab of jealousy for the kind of family life he'd had, the kind of life she'd never known.

"What about you, Maura? Do you have a big family? Any brothers or sisters?" Spencer asked.

Maura hesitated for a second. "No," she said, relieved to see over his shoulder that they were approaching the stables.

"You're an only child. I can't imagine what that's like," he mused. "What about your parents? What does your father do?"

Maura swallowed the lump lodged in her throat. "I didn't know my father. He left before I was born," she said, fighting to keep her tone even.

Spencer caught the faint echo of pain in her voice and another emotion he couldn't quite define. "I'm sorry," he said. "That must have been hard on you and your mother," he commented as he brought Lucifer to a halt in the open paddock adjoining the stables.

"Yes, it was," she replied as she released her hold on Spencer and prepared to dismount.

He offered his hand, but she ignored it, sliding off Lucifer's back onto the ground. The leather saddle creaked as Spencer followed suit.

Joe, the stable hand she'd met earlier, came hurrying toward them.

"Did Stardust made it back all right?" Spencer asked as he handed over Lucifer's reins.

"Yes, sir. The mare came trotting in about ten minutes ago," Joe told them.

"None the worse for wear, I hope," Spencer said.

"Not that I could see," Joe answered.

"A snake spooked her," Spencer explained. "Lucky for us Lucifer didn't make a break for it, as well."

"Ah...excuse me, sir," Joe said, throwing his boss a nervous smile. "Hank wondered if you could take a look at Queenie. He thinks she's bruised her right foreleg."

Concern clouded Spencer's features. "Tell Hank I'll be right there."

Joe nodded and led Lucifer away.

"I have to attend to this," he said to her. "You'll find your way back to the house?"

"No problem," Maura replied.

"I shouldn't be long," he said. "I'll look for those videos when I get there."

"Fine," Maura replied. "I'll see you later."

Maura reached her room without encountering either of her hosts. She tossed her jean jacket on the bed and sat down to tug off her boots. Rising again she crossed to the adjoining bathroom. She washed her hands and as she dried them her gaze shifted to her reflection in the mirror above the vanity.

She was dismayed to still see a faint flush on her cheeks, and she noted, too, that her eyes had a new awareness. Her lips looked fuller, no doubt a lingering effect of Spencer's electrifying kiss.

The memory of those moments swept through her once more. She closed her eyes, reliving the thrill of his mouth on hers, remembering the heat, the excitement and the sudden overwhelming need.

She didn't have much experience when it came to men. And as for kissing, she'd always regarded the obligatory meeting of mouths after a date highly overrated.

Not any longer!

No kiss had ever generated the explosive reaction she'd felt the moment Spencer's lips touched hers. A wave of fresh longing rippled through her, and her breath caught in her throat.

If he were to kiss her again, would he evoke the same overwhelming response?

"Stop it!" Maura spoke the words aloud, effectively breaking out of the daydream. How could she even be thinking about wanting to repeat the kiss?

Maura tossed the towel onto the vanity and returned to the bedroom. Restless, she opened the door leading out onto the small balcony and stepped outside. She took several deep breaths in an effort to oust Spencer from her mind, but like a burr stuck under a saddle she couldn't seem to dislodge him.

What would he think if he knew he'd kissed a twenty-seven-year old virgin? she wondered. He'd probably laugh.

She knew her reluctance to become romantically involved with anyone had stemmed in part from the fact that she'd watched her mother's marriage to Brian O'Sullivan slowly disintegrate. The townsfolk of Bridlewood, old-fashioned in their ways and ideas, had disapproved of the divorce, and not for the first time her mother had become a fresh source of gossip.

Maura could only recall having one date in high school. Stanley Dyer, a quiet spoken but intelligent young man with a mouth full of braces, had asked her to one of the school dances.

When he'd driven her home afterward, his good-night kiss had been rather awkward and Maura could still remember the grating sound of his metal braces scraping against her teeth.

At college her roommate had insisted on arranging double dates, but after spending most of those evenings fighting off clumsy and unwanted advances she'd opted out of the dating scene.

She'd thrown herself into her studies, and kept herself too busy for casual relationships or more serious involvements.

She'd agreed with her mother that an education was important but when she'd returned home with her degree, she'd tossed the certificate in her closet before going out and getting herself a job at one of the stud-horse farms in the area. From that moment on working with horses had been all she'd ever done; all she'd ever wanted. She'd quickly developed a reputation for dealing with troubled or badly behaved horses.

Her first and only long-term relationship had lasted for exactly one month. Raymond Farnsworth had been a decidedly charming and handsome young man, and the nephew of Gerald Farnsworth, owner of one of the biggest stud farms in Kentucky.

Flattered by his attention she'd accepted an invitation to dinner. Much to her surprise she'd enjoyed his company, though when he'd driven her home he hadn't kissed her.

For the next few weeks they'd gone out on a regular basis, but while she'd liked Raymond a lot, his kisses hadn't left her feeling breathless, nor had they sent a thrill of excitement and anticipation racing through her...not like the kiss she'd shared with Spencer.

Maura muttered under her breath. She'd come full circle. Silently she chided herself for allowing one single solitary kiss from a man she wasn't altogether sure she liked to affect her so strongly.

It was unlikely Spencer Diamond would spend any time thinking about her or those moments by the lake. She would simply have to put it out of her mind...forget it ever happened.

Half an hour later when Maura ventured downstairs and into the kitchen, Nora Diamond greeted her with a smile.

"I was just coming to look for you," Nora said. "Spencer called up from the stables and told me to let you know he's been delayed, but that the videos of Indigo you wanted to see are in the den. I hope you know how to run a VCR."

"Yes, I do," Maura assured her, ignoring the stab of disappointment she felt at Spencer's absence.

"Good," Nora said with relief. "I've never quite managed to figure out how they work. Come, I'll show you the den." Nora led the way from the kitchen and down the hall.

"This is Spencer's domain," Nora commented as she opened the first door on the left. "He spends his spare time in here—when he has spare time, that is," she added with a smile.

Maura entered the den and was immediately enfolded by a familiar masculine scent, Spencer's scent, a scent that assaulted her senses inciting a shiver of response.

The room was tastefully decorated in rich autumn shades of orange, green and brown. The carpet was a honey-brown color and the walls a similar tone that had a soothing effect.

Maura liked the fact that the room had an uncluttered look, and she had no problem visualizing Spencer's near-six-foot frame sprawled in the green leather chair. He obviously enjoyed watching television or listening to the impressive collection of CDs shelved on the enormous wall unit built to hold a variety of electronic equipment.

A large-screen television occupied one whole sec-

tion of the wall unit. And Maura could only admire
and envy all the state-of-the-art stereo components
that included a tuner, a tape deck, a disc player as
well as a VCR.

In front of the television sat a beautiful oak coffee
table with glass inlays. On it she could see several
VCR tapes along with three remote control devices.

Two smaller oak and glass tables stood at either
end of a dark-green leather couch, and on the outside
wall was a fireplace made of sandstone.

"Spencer said the tapes of Indigo's race are on
the top shelf," Nora said. "You shouldn't have any
trouble finding them. He prides himself on being
organized."

"Thanks." Maura crossed to the wall unit. "Do
I have time before dinner to watch them?"

"Of course!" Nora smiled and walked toward the
door. "Dinner won't be ready for another hour. I'll
give you a shout."

"If you need any help in the kitchen, I can do
this later," Maura was quick to offer.

"Nonsense. You're here to work with Indigo. Besides, Elliot has everything under control," Nora replied.

After her hostess departed Maura soon located the
tapes of Indigo's last two races. It took a little longer
to figure out which was the remote control for the
machine.

Ten minutes later she sat down on the soft leather
couch and watched Indigo being led toward the
starting gate. As soon as he drew within five feet of

the opening, the powerful Thoroughbred instantly tensed, then proceeded to do everything in his power not to enter the mechanical gate.

Maura watched the racing official grow both angry and impatient until finally Indigo was in the gate. She watched the entire race, enthralled as always by the speed and splendor of the horses galloping to the finish line.

Rewinding the tape, she pressed the play button once again. This time, with the aid of the frame-by-frame feature on the remote control, she watched the fiasco at the starting gate a second time.

She leaned forward, resting her arms on her knees, her attention totally focused on the screen. Once the race was underway she reset the tape to its normal speed. For the second time in as many minutes she watched in admiration as Indigo, left behind in the initial surge from the gates, gradually drew up to the field to catch the leader and sprint past him, reaching the post a full length in front.

The rousing cheer from the racing enthusiasts as Indigo thundered across the finish line drowned out the sound of the door to the den being opened.

"Quite a race, huh?" Spencer commented as he sat down on the couch beside her.

"Oh! You startled me." Maura's heart slammed against her ribs.

"Sorry." Spencer responded, flashing an apologetic smile. "So. What's the verdict?" he asked softly.

Maura drew a ragged breath, willing her racing

pulse to slow down. "He's quite a handful," she replied.

"Not thinking of backing out, are you?"

Maura heard the underlying challenge in Spencer's voice. Though she sensed he still had reservations about her abilities and probably her motives, it was obvious he was willing, at least for Indigo's sake, to give her an opportunity to work with the horse.

A thought flashed into her head. Should she tell Spencer the truth, tell him that Indigo wasn't the only reason she'd come all the way to California?

She was surprised to discover how much she wanted to tell him. But her business was with her father, Michael Carson, the man who'd turned his back on her even before she was born.

She'd come looking for answers, and she wasn't about to walk away until she'd talked to her father, told him who she was and heard what he had to say.

"I came here to try to help Indigo. Why would I want to back out now?" she replied, and tried not to feel guilty when she saw the flicker of admiration and relief that flared briefly in Spencer's eyes.

# Chapter Five

"My father isn't the only one who believes Indigo is a lost cause and that I should withdraw him from racing and put him out to stud." Spencer let his gaze slide to Maura's mouth, his attention lingering for a moment on its seductive fullness.

Suddenly the desire to taste again the exotic flavor that was hers alone almost overwhelmed him, but he reined in the need strumming along his nerve endings.

"It would be a tremendous loss to racing fans not to see him run again," Maura said, managing to maintain at least an outer appearance of calm. In actual fact her heart was pounding against her rib cage in direct response to the flicker of desire she'd just seen in his eyes.

Tension arced between then like an electrical storm waiting to happen. Maura could hardly breathe. What was it about Spencer Diamond that buffeted her senses, igniting a need somewhere deep inside her?

"I totally agree," Spencer said evenly. "So you're going to stay and give it a try?"

At his question a look he couldn't quite decipher flashed briefly in her eyes, and not for the first time he had the impression she was hiding something.

"Yes, I'm staying." Maura replied.

Suddenly a thought struck him. Indigo was a very valuable animal, and security in the racing industry and at the Blue Diamond Ranch was an ongoing concern.

While it might be stretching things a bit, he couldn't entirely rule out the fact that a number of rival owners, not to mention some bookmakers, would be very happy if his multiwinning racehorse could no longer race.

Though his instinct was telling him Maura was hiding something, he had an equally strong feeling that she was sincere in her wish to help Indigo and not undermine his chances of winning. Besides, Indigo was doing a fine job of sabotaging his career all by himself.

But why had she waited two months before calling to offer her help? And why did she seem a tad uneasy around him, like a high-strung filly ready to bolt?

"Tell me something—" he began, but before he could continue the door opened.

"Oh good, you're both here." Nora said as she poked her head into the room. "Dinner's ready!"

Dinner, once again, was a pleasant affair. Conversation flowed easily, thanks to the genuine warmth and friendliness of her hosts.

Recalling Spencer's comments about his brother, Maura asked Nora when her daughter-in-law's baby was expected to arrive.

"Kate isn't due for another two weeks," Nora said. "Sabrina is really excited about having a new baby brother or sister. And we're thrilled, of course, that we'll have another grandchild to spoil." She smiled.

Maura reached for her wineglass and brought it to her lips, all the while thinking yet again what a warm, loving and supportive family the Diamonds were. How she envied Spencer and his siblings for having grown up in the kind of family environment she'd yearned for as a child.

Her thoughts turned to her father. She longed to bring up his name and ask if he'd returned from his trip. But she refrained from making any mention of him, silently hoping he might crop up in the conversation.

After dinner Spencer excused himself and disappeared to his office, saying he had to make a few telephone calls. Maura helped Nora and Elliot clear away the dishes, and soon the kitchen was restored to order.

She declined her hosts' invitation for a stroll around the garden and headed to her room.

When Spencer appeared at the top of the stairs, blocking her path, she felt her stomach muscles clench.

"I'm glad I caught you," he said. "I thought I'd better let you know I'll be leaving early in the morning. I have to drive to San Francisco on business."

"Oh…" Maura said, not sure whether to be relieved or disappointed at the news. She'd assumed Spencer would want to oversee her first session with Indigo…surely he didn't expect her to wait for his return?

"What about Indigo?" she asked. "I should start working with him right away."

"I'm counting on it," he replied promptly. "His next race is a week Saturday. Will that give you enough time to work your magic?" There was a teasing quality to his voice, but Maura heard the underlying concern.

"I'll be better able to tell you what I think after I've had a few sessions with him," Maura responded, knowing that with some horses it could take days or even weeks of intense retraining before any change was made in an animal's behavior.

Spencer nodded. "I've instructed Hank to let you have everything you need, and I also told Joe he'll be working with you."

"Thank you."

Spencer's expression grew serious. "I don't want to put any pressure on you, but I think you should know that there's a lot riding on Indigo and this race.''

Maura noted the faint worry lines creasing the corner of his mouth, and for a breath-robbing moment she wanted to reach out and soothe them away with soft kisses.

At the absurdity of her thoughts, her heart skidded to a halt before stumbling on once more. She forced air into her lungs. ''I can't make you any promises,'' she said, knowing it would be foolish to raise his hopes. ''I'll give you a progress report when you get back.''

Spencer raked a hand through his hair and sighed. ''Thanks,'' he said. Suddenly he flashed a smile that surprised her. ''I don't suppose you'll miss me, will you?'' His tone was light, his eyes twinkling with humor.

Her heartbeat faltered. ''Miss you?'' she repeated, baffled by the swift change in his mood.

He leaned closer, an action that sent her pulse jittering. ''You thought I'd be sitting on the fence breathing down your neck all day, watching your every move, didn't you?''

Spencer's smile widened into a grin that played havoc with her senses. Awareness sizzled through her, and it was all she could do not to respond to his smile.

''Tell me the truth, red. I can take it,'' he went on.

Anger at the use of her nickname bubbled to the surface. ''Don't—'' she began, then abruptly broke off, knowing by the angle of his dark eyebrows that he was baiting her.

"Don't what?" He asked innocently.

"Don't hurry back on my account," she replied rashly, and was rewarded with a low, sexy chuckle, effectively sending her pulse scrambling once more.

Holding her gaze, he brought his hand up to capture a lock of her hair. Though his touch was barely discernible, a white heat shot through her.

"Oh, on the contrary, red. I'll be back as soon as I can," he said, his voice full of promise.

For the next two days Maura spent most of her time with Indigo. When he wasn't out on his regular prerace training regime, she was working with him in the small covered circular track away from the stables.

Her goal was simply to get to know him better, to gain his trust, and that proved to be a challenge. Indigo had grown accustomed to his daily routine, and he made no bones abut the fact that he didn't like changes.

Maura persevered, determined to win his respect. Using a halter and rope she put him through a variety of exercises that quickly confirmed he was indeed a highly intelligent creature and that his perverse reaction had been nothing more than a test— a test she was determined to pass.

By late afternoon on the first day Maura had Joe bring the truck and trailer into the yard. From the moment Indigo saw the trailer, Maura immediately sensed his anxiety level rise a notch.

Maura made no move to lead Indigo up the ramp. Instead she walked him around both vehicles a number of times, letting him have a good, long look at their size and shape without ever taking him near the ramp.

After a little while Indigo began to relax, walking past the ramp with nothing more than a flick of his tail. Maura continued to walk him around the vehicles before instructing Joe, who'd been standing nearby, to drive the trailer away.

By midafternoon on the second day Indigo seemed to be enjoying himself, deciding that he liked the extra attention he was receiving. After she'd put him through the same exercises as the day before, Maura decided it was time to load him into the horse trailer.

Joe drove the truck and trailer into the yard, then lowered the ramp. He moved away to watch on the sidelines, and once again Maura began to walk Indigo around the vehicles, watching and waiting for a reaction.

On the fourth go-around Maura changed tactics and led Indigo straight toward the ramp. Indigo began to nod his head and tug at his halter, but Maura held on firmly, paying no attention. She continued to lead him up the ramp, all the while speaking softly and encouragingly.

Moments later he was inside the box. Joe ran to close it, but Maura shook her head signaling to him not to bother. She patted Indigo, praising him for his accomplishment, before walking him down the ramp.

For the next ten minutes she walked him around the vehicles and up and down the ramp, until she was satisfied the ramp and the trailer no longer held any threat for him.

"You can put the horse box away," Maura said when she reached the bottom of the ramp.

"Right, miss," Joe replied. "Nice work. Well done," he added with a smile.

"Thanks." Maura said before Joe headed toward the front of the truck.

"Good boy," Maura told Indigo as she patted his neck.

"I see you're making progress." The sound of Spencer's deep voice jolted her.

She turned to see his tall handsome figure walking toward her. A smile played over his face, sending a flurry of emotion rippling through her.

For the past two days she'd worked hard to push all thoughts of him aside in order to focus on Indigo. But one glimpse of Spencer and her senses were suddenly veering off course.

Beside her, Indigo, no doubt recognizing the scent of his owner, nickered in welcome.

"Hello there, big fella." Spencer reached out to rub Indigo's nose before turning his blue gaze on Maura. "Dad told me he's hardly seen you since I left," he commented. "If what I just witnessed is anything to go by, I'd say your particular brand of magic appears to be working."

"Thank you," she said, warmed by his words. "It's a start, but we still have a long way to go. I haven't taken him anywhere near a starting gate yet." Tension hummed through her, and she was glad Indigo stood like a wall of defense between them.

"I have every confidence you'll succeed," Spencer said.

Maura laughed and shook her head, loosening a few strands of hair from their confines. "Liar! At least that's not what I heard you say in Kentucky." She was surprised at her own boldness.

Spencer's eyes narrowed. "Ah...so you did overhear me spouting off. I *thought* from your reaction that night you must have been eavesdropping. Was that reason you refused my initial invitation?"

"You were very rude," Maura told him.

"You're right, I was," he replied, and Maura caught the glimmer of amusement lurking in the depths of his blue eyes. "Overdue though it is, I hope you'll accept my apologies."

"Of course," Maura replied, silently acknowledging his easy charm. "Now if you'll excuse me, Indigo deserves his supper and a good brush down."

"He does indeed, but you look as if you could use a break, yourself," he said. "Here's Joe. He'll take care of Indigo."

Maura turned to see the stable hand approaching. Though she wanted to tell Spencer she'd rather stay with Indigo, she smiled at Joe as she reluctantly handed him the lead rope.

"Night, boy. I'll see you in the morning." She gave the horse's neck one last rub before falling into step beside Spencer.

As they took the path leading to the security gate, Spencer noted the dust on Maura's shirt and jeans as well as a few smudges of dirt on her face.

Her coppery hair was slowly unraveling from the tight braid she favored, and Spencer had to fight the urge to reach out and liberate the rest of the curls already attempting to escape.

He'd been amazed how often during the past forty-eight hours her tantalizing image had drifting into his mind. But what surprised him more was how readily he could bring to mind the hot taste of her and the way her body had felt crushed under his.

It had been a long time since any woman had intrigued him or aroused such a strong response. But he couldn't quite shake the feeling that she was hiding something.

If there was one thing he couldn't tolerate it was deception. Deceit had been at the root of his problems with Lucy, and he still berated himself for being blind to her faults. She lied about everything, about loving him, about wanting his baby.

When he'd realized the truth, he'd been stunned and disgusted. She'd kept her secret well, concealing the truth from everyone, including her parents.

"How was your trip to San Francisco?" Maura asked, breaking the silence.

Spencer gladly dragged his thoughts away from Lucy. "Very successful," he replied as they reached the security gate. He punched in the code and opened the gate.

"Thank you." Maura ducked under his arm.

They were silent until they reached the veranda. With his hand on the kitchen door Spencer turned to her.

"Oh...I should tell you we have a visitor. We were talking about him at dinner the other night.

"He's our neighbor, Michael Carson."

# Chapter Six

Maura felt the blood drain from her face. Though she'd been hoping her father would pay the Diamonds a visit, now that he was here she was suddenly swamped with feelings of uncertainty and excitement.

"Yes...I remember," Maura replied with a casualness she was far from feeling. Her mouth was dry, her hands damp with perspiration, and she had to fight to conceal the turmoil raging inside.

She was intensely aware of Spencer's steady gaze on her. He'd deliberately waited until the last minute to tell her of Michael Carson's visit, of that she was sure, no doubt wanting to catch her unawares and gauge her reaction.

"He's been suffering from jet lag," Spencer said.

Maura curved her mouth into a semblance of a smile. "That's right, he was in the Caribbean on a cruise, wasn't he?'' she said, pretending she'd only just remembered the fact, when in reality she'd memorized every detail concerning her father.

"Yes," Spencer replied. "I've told him all about you. He's dying to meet you." He smiled as he opened the door leading to the kitchen.

Maura swallowed convulsively. The prospect of coming face-to-face with the man she believed was her father sent her pulse skyrocketing and left her feeling weak at the knees.

She moved past Spencer through the open doorway, wondering if he could hear the thunderous roar of her heartbeat.

Once inside, she came to a halt. She could see three people seated at the kitchen table. They all turned toward her, and Maura's heart lodged in her throat when her gaze came to rest on the neatly dressed stranger seated with his back to the window—the stranger who was her father.

She could hear the blood pounding inside her head as she took in his handsome features, his silver hair, gray eyes and slightly gaunt face.

"There you are." Nora rose from the table. "Maura, come and meet our neighbor and friend, Michael Carson."

Maura's cheeks ached from the effort to keep smiling. With a concentrated effort she crossed the floor, each step taking her closer to the man she never knew existed until a few weeks ago.

"Michael, this is Maura O'Sullivan," Nora went on. "She's helping Spencer work with Indigo."

Michael Carson rose and came around the table to greet her.

"Maura, what a lovely name. It's a pleasure to meet you," he said extending his hand.

"Thank you." Maura's voice was husky with suppressed emotion. Inside she was shaking like a leaf in a gale, and she hoped no one noticed that as she reached for her father's hand her own was trembling.

The clasp of hands was fleeting, but as their eyes met Maura thought she saw a flicker of something, recognition, in her father's eyes. She'd often been told she looked like her mother. Had Michael seen the resemblance?

The tension inside her stretched to near breaking point. Her mind was suddenly jammed with the questions she wanted to ask. But when she saw his smile fade and his expression change to a frown, disappointment slammed into her. She swayed.

Spencer instantly came up behind her, placing his arm around her for support. "Are you all right?" he asked.

"It's nothing, I'm fine." Maura insisted, but her tone lacked conviction. "I'm sorry. I guess I'm a little hungry, that's all," she said quickly, giving the only excuse she could think of.

She eased away from Spencer, finding that his touch merely compounded the dizziness assailing her. "I...ah...I didn't stop for lunch." She spoke haltingly, praying the explanation would allay his suspicions, but one glance at Spencer's face told her she hadn't succeeded.

"Skipping meals isn't healthy," Nora scolded in a motherly tone. "Come and sit down, Maura. There's a plate of cheese and crackers on the table. Have some."

It was a relief to sit. Her body and mind were battling to cope with the onslaught of emotions still threatening to drag her under.

Spencer leaned over to pull the plate of cheese and crackers toward her.

Beside her Michael plucked a napkin from the napkin holder and offered it to her.

"Thank you," she mumbled, managing a smile.

"Eat." The order came from Spencer. His breath fanned her ear, sending a shiver through her. She picked up a cracker and bit into it. It tasted like dust in her mouth, and she had to fight to control a fresh wave of nausea.

Nora, who'd risen and gone to the fridge, came around the counter carrying a glass of orange juice. She set it down on the table in front of Maura. "Drink this. It'll help." Nora ordered with an encouraging smile.

Maura mumbled her thanks, painfully aware of everyone's eyes on her. She knew she was dangerously close to tears, and she silently wished she could wave a magic wand and make them all disappear...all except her father.

She picked up the glass of juice and swallowed

several small mouthfuls. To her surprise the cool, sweet liquid seemed to steady her a little.

"Hmm...that feels better," she said summoning up a smile.

She glanced at her father, and her stomach muscles tightened. "I hear you were on a cruise," she said, wanting to direct the attention elsewhere. "How was it?" she asked, relieved that her voice sounded normal.

"Very nice," he replied.

"Michael was just telling us about the beautiful San Blas Islands," Nora chimed in.

"Oh. Where are they?" Maura asked.

"They are a group of small islands in the Caribbean Sea a few miles off the north coast of Panama," Michael replied. "The ship drops anchor and native people paddle out to it in their dugout canoes or small boats.

"It's quite a sight," he added with a smile. "They surround the ship, and start chanting 'money, money, money,' hoping the passengers out on deck will throw coins down to them," he explained. "They even use upturned umbrellas to catch whatever is thrown. The crew discourages everyone from taking part, but it's a colorful scene, nonetheless." His gaze turned to Maura. "Spencer tells me you're from Kentucky."

"Yes, I'm from a small town near Lexington," she replied. A new tension shimmered through her as she watched for his reaction.

"I visited the Lexington area years ago," her father said. "The surrounding countryside is quite beautiful if I recall," he added with a smile.

Maura tried to appear casual as she let her gaze drift slowly over his face, memorizing every detail. She could see shadows under his eyes.

She guessed his age to be somewhere in the mid-sixties. He was a handsome man, and Maura could easily understand how her mother would have found him attractive.

"How long ago was that?" Maura asked, hoping he might say something that would verify his having met her mother.

"Oh…it must be over twenty-five years ago, maybe longer. Yes, more like twenty-eight. It's hard to believe," he said with a shake of his head. "I can't quite recall why I was there." He frowned. "Wait…yes, that was when I—" He abruptly broke off, and Maura watched as his expression turned serious, and a hint of sorrow clouded his eyes.

Maura's heartbeat quickened. Was he remembering her mother? She wondered. How she longed to ask him, desperate to know if Bridget Murphy, the woman who'd given him both her body and her heart so many years ago, held any place in his heart.

"Was Ruth with you on that trip?" Elliot asked, cutting through the silence.

At the mention of his wife's name, Michael blinked and drew a breath. "No…. No, Ruth and I weren't married then." Distracted, he glanced at his wristwatch. "Elliot, look at the time. We'd better get going."

"You're right," Nora said before turning to Maura. "Maura, I'm sorry to spring this on you without warning, but we haven't seen you all day," she went on. "It's just that every other Friday night a group of our retired friends get together for dinner at the golf club, followed by a few hands of bridge," she explained.

"Don't worry, I'll be fine," Maura quickly assured her.

"Of course you will," Nora said with a smile. "I told Spencer he must take you out somewhere nice for dinner."

Maura's heart dropped. "There's really no need."

"Nonsense!" came the reply. "Besides, cooking was never one of Spencer's strong points," she added.

"Thank you for that wonderful testimonial, Mother." Spencer's grin was a little lopsided.

"Well, it's true," his mother responded unabashed.

"Come on, dear," Elliot urged.

"Have a nice evening," Maura said, rising from the table.

"It was a pleasure to meet you, Maura," Michael Carson said. "I'll look forward to seeing you again."

"Me, too," she said and watched as he followed Elliot and Nora from the room.

Left alone with Spencer, Maura could feel his eyes on her. The silence stretched for several long seconds, the air filling with a new and different tension.

From the moment she'd entered the kitchen he'd been watching her closely, and she felt sure that he hadn't bought her explanation that lack of food had been the reason for her near faint.

She tensed in anticipation of the questions she was sure he would ask, questions she wasn't ready to answer. Because until she could talk to her father alone, and establish whether or not he cared or was remotely interested in the fact that she was his daughter, she would keep her own counsel.

"What's your favorite type of food?" Spencer asked.

Surprised and a little wary, Maura glanced at him.

"You don't have to take me out for dinner," she said. "You probably have much more important things to do. I can easily cook something up for myself," she added.

"I'm sure you could," he said with a smile. "But as for having more important things to do—well, there's nothing more important to me right now than hearing about Indigo and the progress you've made so far.

"Besides, my mother would never forgive me if she found out I'd reneged on my promise and that you spent the evening slaving in the kitchen."

"I won't tell her, if you won't," Maura countered in a last-ditch effort to dissuade him.

Spencer grinned. "Nice try, but trust me, mothers have a way of finding out these things. So in order to save my hide, meet me in the front hall in…let's say, half an hour?''

Maura met his gaze. The determined gleam in his blue eyes told her it would be futile to argue.

"Half an hour," she repeated before making her escape.

Twenty minutes later Spencer stood at the foot of the stairs waiting for Maura. He was still puzzling over her strange reaction when he'd told her Michael Carson was inside.

He'd watched the blood drain from her face leaving her looking pale and forlorn, but what had puzzled him more had been the look of uncertainty mixed with a flash of joy he'd seen in her eyes.

Did Maura know Michael? Had they met before? It seemed highly unlikely, especially after Michael's comment that he hadn't been to Kentucky in more than twenty-five years.

But he recalled that Hank, his stable manager, had mentioned that Maura had been asking about Michael. Why would she ask the stable hands about their neighbor?

Spencer was going solely on gut instinct, the same instinct he'd chosen to ignore when it came to his wife's erratic behavior.

Spencer sighed. He should have realized much sooner that something was wrong with Lucy. He should have read the signs, known by her often dramatic mood swings and quick temper that it was more than just that she was spoiled and reckless.

In hindsight he acknowledged that he hadn't wanted to believe the woman he thought he loved, the woman he'd asked to be his wife and bear his children had gone to such lengths to deprive him of the family he so wanted.

He'd always had a soft spot for Lucy, the daughter of his parents' best friends, for as long as he could remember.

She'd grown up wanting for nothing. After dropping out of college with the explanation that she wasn't ready to choose a career, her parents—or more rightly, her mother—had indulged her, sending her off to Europe so she could explore and absorb its beauty and history.

When Lucy returned from her travels, Spencer had attended a big welcome-home party put on by Michael and Ruth. Lucy had looked decidedly sexy, sporting a dazzling new hairstyle and snazzy clothes. She'd developed an air of sophistication and confidence that had stirred his senses, and he'd been astonished to discover the feelings she aroused in him.

Both families had been pleased when they'd started dating, and when he'd overheard his mother talking to a friend about the possibility of wedding bells and more grandchildren, he'd found himself liking the idea.

Settling down and raising a family had enormous appeal, and he could easily picture Lucy in the role of wife and mother. They'd been married six months later.

While he'd acknowledged that Lucy had always enjoyed an active social life, that she liked to be the center of attention, he'd hoped in time she would slowly wind down those activities and think about starting a family.

But shortly after their return from a honeymoon in Mexico, Lucy went back to her partying ways, ignoring his requests to stay home. His own busy work schedule at the time hadn't helped matters, and it had become something of a habit to meet her friends without him.

When Spencer confronted her and suggested she cut down on these outings, Lucy had yelled at him, then cried, telling him she was bored sitting around the ranch house.

Her behavior had become erratic, her mood swings worsened, but he'd been involved in a business deal that promised to bring several new clients his way, and he'd ignored his instincts.

One afternoon, determined to find out what was troubling Lucy, he'd returned to the house early, hoping to talk to her. That's when he'd found her on the bathroom floor, bleeding heavily.

He'd taken her to emergency where he'd learned that the hemorrhage had been the aftermath of an abortion. That's when he'd had to face the truth— their marriage was in far deeper trouble than he'd ever imagined.

"I'm sorry! I hope I haven't kept you waiting." Maura's voice cut through Spencer's musings. Pushing thoughts of Lucy aside, he turned to watch Maura descend the few remaining steps.

She wore the same rainbow-colored skirt, but in place of her cream blouse was a short-sleeved, black-knit top that hugged her figure like a second skin, accentuating the gentle swell of her breasts.

Her hair was tamed once more, twisted into a severe knot at the base of her neck with only a few wispy curls framing her heart-shaped face.

Not for the first time Spencer felt the urge to haul the pins from her hair and spear his hands through the coppery red tresses before planting a kiss on her lips that would rattle her composure the way she rattled his.

"It was definitely worth the wait," he told her. "May I say, you look lovely."

Maura moistened lips that were suddenly dry. "Thank you," she managed to say, totally disconcerted by the compliment spoken so sincerely.

She felt a blush creep up her cheeks, and she knew by the glint of amusement in Spencer's blue eyes that it hadn't gone unnoticed.

"Shall we go?"

# Chapter Seven

"**I** hope you like Italian food," Spencer said twenty minutes later, when he made the turn onto what appeared to be a main thoroughfare.

"I love it," she replied.

"In case you're wondering, this is Kincade's Main Street," he told her, confirming her guess. "It looks like they're already starting to put the decorations up for our Easter Parade."

Maura saw a number of colorful flags and ribbons hanging from several lamp standards.

"You have an Easter Parade?"

"Yes. It's a tradition around here," he said. "The parade itself starts at the other end of town, then follows a route that brings it down Main Street."

"It must be a big celebration," she said, knowing that there were some communities that put a good deal of time, effort and money into such events.

"One of the biggest," he said. "Marching bands from all the high schools in the surrounding area compete for trophies and other prizes, and the winner takes pride of place leading off the parade." He flashed a smile.

"And there's also a flotilla of decorated floats," he continued. "Some come from as far away as Oregon and Washington. One of the popular attractions in the parade is an old covered wagon pulled by four horses. You might enjoy that."

"That *would* be a treat to see," Maura commented. "You say it's local?"

"Yes. The wagon is one of two that belong to our neighbor, Michael Carson," Spencer explained.

"Mi— Mr. Carson owns the covered wagon?" she repeated, unable to hide her surprise.

Spencer nodded. "Every Easter, for as far back as I can remember, Michael has been a major contributor to the parade. He's the one I was telling you about, the one who collects Western memorabilia."

"Really!" Maura said, recalling that Spencer had mentioned knowing someone with an interest in the early pioneer days. The realization that he'd been talking about her father and that they had a shared interest brought a flood of warmth to her heart.

"When my brother and I were growing up, Mother would dress us up in cowboy garb and, depending on how old we were, we'd ride in the wagon or on horseback behind it." He laughed softly at the memory.

"That must have been fun," Maura commented, with a stab of envy.

"We looked forward to it every year," Spencer replied. "Ah...here we are." He pulled into a parking lot.

"This is a busy spot," Maura said, noting that the lot was nearly full.

"Dimitri's is very popular on weekends," he acknowledged. "It helps that the trio who perform are great. And the dance floor adds to the attraction." He switched off the engine and reached for the door handle.

"Dance floor?" Maura repeated, as a flicker of alarm chased through her.

Spencer came around to the passenger side of the car and opened the door. "You do know how to dance, don't you?" He asked as he held out his hand to her.

Maura ignored his outstretched hand and climbed out unassisted. "Yes, I can dance, but I—"

"Good," Spencer responded cutting her off in mid-sentence. "But first I think we should eat," he went on. "I called before we left and made a reservation."

Maura fell into step beside him, wishing she'd insisted on staying at the ranch. She couldn't tell if he was merely teasing her, but the thought of dancing with Spencer was doing strange things to her pulse.

Once they were inside the restaurant, an attractive

young woman with short blond hair came forward to greet them.

"Hello, Kelly," Spencer said. "How are you?"

"Fine thank you, Mr. Diamond," the girl replied, her gaze lingering appreciatively on Spencer.

"I believe you have a table for us," he said.

"Yes, of course. If you'll come this way." Grabbing two menus from the counter, Kelly led them into the dining area.

Maura scanned the spacious restaurant as she followed the young woman. Most of the tables were already occupied, and the low buzz of conversation echoed around the room.

A tantalizing smell of spaghetti sauce, melted cheese and garlic, as well as other enticing aromas, filled the air, adding to the ambience and making her mouth water.

In the small area on the other side of the dance floor stood two large speakers, an electric keyboard and a set of drums. There was no sign of the trio of musicians Spencer had mentioned.

Crisp white tablecloths draped the tables. At the center stood a tall candle and a bud vase with a single red carnation. Kelly, their hostess, came to a halt not far from the dance floor.

Once they were seated, Kelly handed Maura and Spencer menus, then filled their water glasses. "Have a nice evening," she said and withdrew.

Maura opened the leather-bound menu and tried to concentrate on the items listed. Had Spencer been serious? Was he really going to ask her to dance?

Just the thought of being in his arms, their bodies touching, sent a ripple of need through her. Not for the first time, Maura wondered what it was about Spencer that affected her so strongly.

She lowered her menu a little to peek at him. Their glances collided, and instantly her heart careened against her ribs in reaction.

"Have you decided?" he asked.

"Ah...no." She dropped her gaze back to the menu, but the words seemed to converge into a jumble of letters.

"I recommend the seafood cannelloni—it's one of my favorites," Spencer said. "The lasagna is also very good, and their spaghetti and meatballs are the best in town."

Maura closed the menu and managed a smile. "They all sound wonderful," she replied. "I think I'll try the cannelloni."

"Excellent choice," he said. "And what about a Caesar salad to start things off?"

"That would be lovely, thank you," Maura replied thinking that anyone watching might mistakenly think they were on a date.

She reached for the water glass in the hope that the ice-cold liquid would somehow alleviate the tension slowly tightening like a vise inside her. It had been a long time since she'd dated anyone. Nursing her mother through her long illness had left her little time for herself.

When the waiter appeared Spencer placed their order while Maura let her gaze travel around the room once more. She noticed two men and a tall, dark-haired woman wearing a sequined navy dress making their way toward the instruments in the corner.

"Would you like a glass of wine?" Spencer asked, capturing her attention.

"No, thank you, I'll pass," she responded, deciding that his presence was quite intoxicating enough.

"So, tell me more about yourself," Spencer invited once the waiter had departed.

Maura met his gaze, silently acknowledging that Spencer Diamond was by far the most attractive man she'd ever met. She swallowed nervously. "There's really not much to tell."

Spencer leaned forward, resting his forearms on the edge of the table. "If there's nothing to tell, then let me hazard a few guesses. With the name O'Sullivan you must have some Irish blood in you."

"Yes, I am part Irish," she confessed.

"Which part?" he asked, his voice teasing, his smile widening to show a row of even white teeth.

Maura laughed, unable to resist the humor lurking in the depths of those amazing blue eyes.

"Definitely your hair," he went on, his gaze appreciative. "Has anyone ever told you have beautiful hair?"

Her breath caught in her throat at the simple but sincere compliment. "No, and thank you," she managed to say aware of a heat spreading through her. "I'm actually Irish on my mother's side," she volunteered.

"Not your father's?" Spencer said.

Maura dropped her gaze. Reaching for the water glass she took a sip.

"O'Sullivan was my stepfather's name," she told him. "He adopted me when he married my mother. They broke up a few years later."

"That's right, I remember, you said your real father left before you were born," Spencer commented. "Did your mother ever tell you why he left?"

Before Maura could answer, a busboy set a small basket of buns on the table. Moments later the first bars of a familiar love song filled the room as the trio began to play.

Maura turned toward the sound. The woman she'd seen walking toward the stage now stood in front of the microphone. She started to sing, her voice low and seductive as she pleaded with her lover to return.

Several couples rose from nearby tables and crossed to the tiny dance floor.

"She has quite a voice," Maura said, relieved to be able to use the interruption to shift the conversation away from herself and her father.

"Yes, she does," Spencer agreed as the waiter appeared with their salads.

Throughout the meal Maura managed to keep the conversation on more general topics, and she readily answered his questions about her progress with Indigo.

The trio of musicians continued to entertain the

dinner crowd, and Maura noted that the dance floor was rarely empty.

"How about dessert, or coffee, perhaps?" Spencer asked, once the waiter had removed their plates.

"Coffee, please," Maura replied with a smile. "The meal was delicious. Thank you," she added.

"My pleasure," he said. "But the evening isn't over. We must be the only two people who haven't taken a turn on the dance floor. I think we should remedy that, don't you?" His smile was inviting, and Maura felt her heart skip a beat.

"I really—" she began.

"You did say you could dance?" Spencer said as he stood up.

She hesitated. "Yes, but I—"

"I promise I won't step on your toes," he teased.

Maura lifted her gaze to meet his. There was no mistaking the gleam of challenge in his eyes. Summoning her courage, she rose and walked ahead of Spencer to the dance floor.

The music playing was another soul-wrenching ballad about someone breaking someone's heart. Reaching the parquet floor, Maura turned to Spencer and seconds later she was in his arms.

As their bodies made contact, a multitude of tiny explosions erupted inside her, effectively stealing the breath from her lungs. Her skin tingled as if she'd come in contact with an electric current and the heat spiraling through her was leaving a trail of need in its wake.

Spencer closed his eyes and listened to the seductive beat of the music. Silently he admitted that he'd deliberately chosen this restaurant for the simple reason he wanted to feel her in his arms again.

Maura's body fitted perfectly against his, and it was all he could do not to nibble on the delicate lobe of her ear or plant a row of kisses down her slender neck. Every step, every move, ignited a fire that threatened to consume him.

The scent of wildflowers and springtime assailed him, and when he felt an almost imperceptible shiver vibrate through her, it was gratifying to know she was equally as disturbed as he.

Being in Spencer's arms was more seductive than she'd imagined. Every cell, every nerve, seemed to be attuned to the man holding her. His masculine scent filled her senses, heightening her awareness of his lean, muscular body pressed against hers.

It was almost as if they'd been dance partners for years instead of a few short minutes. She anticipated every step, every turn, her feet seeming scarcely to touch the floor, and she silently prayed the song would never end.

But the music slowly faded and died, and Maura had to bite back a moan of disappointment when he slowly released her.

"That wasn't too bad was it?" Spencer asked, his voice faintly husky.

Maura could only nod. With his hand lightly touching her back, he guided her to the table.

After they'd resumed their seats, the waiter appeared, carrying two cups of coffee.

Spencer watched in silence as Maura added cream to her coffee. Her face was flushed, her mouth soft and sensual, and the urge to taste her again was almost more than he could resist.

He tried to tell himself that the reason she aroused such a strong physical reaction was simply because for the past two years, since Lucy's death, he'd been leading a celibate life. But he knew he was fooling himself.

What was it about Maura that drew him like a magnet, awakening needs he hadn't felt in a long time?

She was beautiful, stunningly so in fact, and intelligent. And she'd earned his respect for the way she'd handled Indigo.

But...

Somehow he couldn't quite dismiss the notion that she was hiding something...that she had another reason for being in Kincade, one he had every intention of uncovering.

He took a sip of coffee. "You still haven't told me much about yourself." He leaned back in his chair and studied her. "Let's see...I know you're an only child...that your mother was Irish...you never knew your father and that you have a way with horses." He paused and frowned. "What about relationships? Is there a lover pining for you back in Kentucky?"

Maura was startled by his question.

"That's rather a personal question. I'm not sure it's any of your business," she replied calmly.

His smile flashed. "So, there's no lover, no boyfriend, no husband," he countered without missing a beat.

For a fleeting moment Maura was sorely tempted to lie, to tell him that she had several lovers, a whole houseful in fact, just to see his reaction.

"As I said, it's none of your business," she repeated, gritting her teeth when she saw his smile widen.

"What about you, Spencer?" she continued, irked enough to want to turn the tables on him. "Is there a woman in your life? Or are you still grieving over your wife?"

His pupils darkened to a midnight-blue, and an emotion she couldn't decipher flickered in their depths before he quickly controlled it. Maura instantly regretted her words.

"I'm sorry. That was rude and insensitive of me," she added.

"Don't apologize, I deserved it," he acknowledged graciously. "And you're right, your personal life is none of my business."

"Would you like more coffee?" The waiter's presence effectively dispelled the tension.

"No, thank you." They replied in unison.

"Bring me the bill, please," Spencer said.

"Excuse me, I'll be right back." Maura rose and headed to the ladies' room.

Spencer sat waiting for Maura to return. She'd had every right to be annoyed with him, but for reasons he wasn't sure he was ready to acknowledge, he'd wanted to know if she was already involved in a relationship.

He admired the way she'd stood up to him, refusing to answer, but he was reasonably sure he was right. However, her question about whether he was still grieving had caught him off guard.

Spencer spotted Maura approaching. He stood up and met her halfway. She made no comment as they walked back to the car.

As he pulled out of the parking lot his thoughts turned to Lucy. He still harbored a good deal of guilt, believing that if he hadn't been embroiled in business, hadn't ignored his instincts, that if he'd only paid more attention to his wife he would have realized sooner she was hiding something.

On her return from her extended trip to Europe, he'd fallen in love with the new, confident and sexy Lucy. He'd trusted her, believing his love had been returned, that they'd held the same dreams of having a family.

It had been a hard pill to swallow to learn that she'd deliberately destroyed the child they'd created simply to retain the life-style she enjoyed.

And it had been a hard truth to face that the woman he'd thought he loved had been nothing more than a shallow, self-centered, spoiled child. He was grateful both his and Lucy's parents had been away at the time. He hadn't had the heart to tell Ruth and Michael what their daughter had done.

When she'd been released from hospital two days later, he'd tried to talk to her, to ask her why she hadn't bothered to tell him about the baby. She'd told him quite bluntly that she didn't want children, had never wanted them, that she had no intention of spoiling her figure for him or for anyone.

An hour later she'd stormed out of the house and into her car. She'd missed the entrance ramp to the freeway, slamming into a wall of concrete.

Spencer clamped down on the feelings of anguish and despair suddenly threatening to resurface.

He drove around to the rear of the house and pulled up next to the garage.

"Thanks again for a lovely dinner," Maura said as they climbed the back stairs to the veranda.

"No problem," he replied. "It's such a beautiful night, perfect for sitting on the porch-swing and counting the stars. What do you say?" he asked, wanting to prolong the evening.

Maura pondered the invitation. Throughout the journey home Spencer hadn't said as much as one word. She felt sure he'd been thinking about his wife and she felt a fresh stab of envy for her half-sister Lucy, the woman who'd been lucky enough to win the heart of a man like Spencer Diamond.

The temperature had cooled, but not unpleasantly, and up in the night sky the stars twinkled invitingly. She wasn't tired and she knew she would only lie awake.

"That sounds nice, thank you," she replied, hoping she wouldn't regret her decision.

When they reached the top Spencer ushered her toward the swing. "Have a seat. Start counting the stars. I'll be right back,'' he said as he unlocked the kitchen door and slipped inside.

Maura wandered over to the wooden rail and stood gazing out over the roofs of the stables that were the Blue Diamond Ranch. Not for the first time she wondered how different her life would have been had her mother moved to California and married Michael Carson.

During the brief but memorable meeting she'd had with her father, she'd found him charming and friendly and it was no secret that he was loved and respected by the Diamond family.

But as he'd talked about Kentucky, he'd stopped suddenly as if he'd remembered something...or someone. She would have liked to pursue the matter and ask him if he'd recalled meeting her mother, but she felt strongly that it was a private matter.

Much as she needed to know, for her own peace of mind why he'd turned his back on her mother and their unborn child, the answers would have to wait.

That hadn't stopped her speculating on just what his reason had been. She'd come up with several, neither of which showed her father in a good light.

Perhaps he'd simply been a playboy who'd seduced her mother then returned to California leaving her to bear the consequences of her actions alone.

Maybe he'd been the kind of man who'd lied to a young and impressionable Bridget Murphy simply to get her into his bed. Or was there another less damning explanation, one that was understandable, even forgivable.

"You're supposed to be counting stars." Spencer's teasing tone cut through her musings.

She smiled and shook her head. "There's way too many," she said, and felt a shiver chase down her spine as his dark masculine scent assailed her.

"Why don't we sit down," Spencer suggested.

Maura crossed to the old wooden swing and sat down.

"There's something I've been meaning to ask," Spencer said as he joined her.

"Fire away," Maura said, thinking he must have a question concerning her work with Indigo.

"Why have you been asking Jo and Hank questions about Michael Carson?"

# *Chapter Eight*

Spencer watched Maura's eyes widen with shock. She stared at him for several seconds before dropping her gaze, but not before he'd seen a look of guilt flash briefly in the depths of her hazel eyes.

"I don't know what you mean," Maura said, but while her voice had an edge to it, her tone lacked conviction.

"I think you do," Spencer replied noting her reluctance to meet his gaze.

Spencer's question had thrown her for a loop. The realization that he'd asked Hank to keep an eye on her stung. How else would he have known she'd been asking questions about her father?

He didn't trust her, that much was clear, and she was surprised to discover how much that hurt.

"I told you. I'm here to work with Indigo," Maura said with a calmness she was far from feeling. "I was merely making conversation with Hank."

"Why don't I believe you?" Spencer asked, annoyance in his voice. He pushed off the swing and stood up.

Maura slowed the swing's sudden movement with her feet. The evening had grown cold. She shivered as she too got to her feet.

"If you want me to leave, I will," she said, silently praying it wouldn't come to that.

Spencer spun around to face her.

"No! Damn it! I don't want you to leave," Spencer muttered. Even under the muted lighting on the veranda she could see frustration as well as another emotion, less easy to decipher, in his eyes.

The urge to confide in him, to tell him the truth and ease the tension she could see on his handsome face almost overwhelmed her. But she bit back the explanation hovering on her lips.

She understood and even admired Spencer's impulse to protect the man who'd been his father-in-law, a man he obviously held in high regard. But until such time as she had an opportunity to talk to her father and find out his feelings on her paternity, she was determined to keep the matter private.

The possibility that Michael Carson would deny he was her father and turn his back on her was very real and not to be ignored. She was simply trying to safeguard her own heart should he reject her a second time.

"There *is* something, isn't there?" he persisted.

Maura met his piercing gaze and felt her heart slam against her breastbone in reaction.

"Nothing that should concern you," she said, knowing she was saying too much, but hoping it would be enough to satisfy him. "I think I'll go in now." She made a move toward the back door.

She didn't get far. His hands snaked out to stop her. He grabbed her upper arms almost as if he might shake her. His touch sent a frisson of alarm and awareness through her and it was all she could do to meet his gaze.

His blue eyes looked deeply into hers, holding her captive.

"Spencer, please..." she started to say, but her words were cut off in midsentence when his mouth came down on hers.

The kiss was hot, wet and punishing. Maura's response was instant as sensation after sensation washed over her, sweeping aside any resistance and leaving a trail of desire in its wake.

She hadn't realized how much she'd wanted him to kiss her again, until now. The heat, the fire, the need spiraled through her, igniting every nerve, every cell to glorious life.

She couldn't seem to get enough. His mouth, at once urgent and demanding, softened to tease and tantalize, enticing her closer and closer to the edge of reason. With only the power of his kisses, he'd aroused a desire so strong she sensed only his physical possession could assuage it.

So this was desire, this all-consuming and clamoring need to feel his naked body next to hers, to explore its masculine mysteries and to surrender her feminine ones into his safekeeping and make that final leap into womanhood.

Spencer was on fire. Hot flames of desire were threatening to consume him, and his only thought was that he wanted to wrap himself in her fiery heat and lose himself totally in her body forever.

Passion, the likes of which he'd never felt before, tore through him like a tornado through a forest, uprooting everything in its path.

It had never been like this before...not even with Lucy.

The thought of Lucy acted like a splash of ice-cold water, effectively dousing the blazing fire and bringing him to his senses. He broke the electrifying kiss and took an unsteady step backward.

Maura's arms dropped to her sides, and as he studied her face, a bruised look came into her eyes. His gaze was drawn to her lips, swollen and still moist from his kisses, and he could hear his heart thundering in his ears as he fought against the urge to haul her back into his arms.

"Not again...never again," he said. Spinning away, he strode across the veranda and down the stairs into the night.

Maura lay awake long into the night, disturbed not only by the devastating kiss, but by the words Spencer had spoken before he stormed off. While she could understand his anger and frustration at her stubborn refusal to explain, she couldn't understand his comment—*Not again, never again.* What had he meant?

By the time she drifted off to sleep, she'd made a vow to try as much as possible to stay out of Spencer's way. Once she fulfilled her obligation to help Indigo overcome his fear of starting gates, once her work was over, she would she move into town and somehow arrange to meet privately with her father.

For the next five days Maura maintained a rigid schedule. Other than seeing Spencer at the dinner table each night, she managed to keep their encounters to a minimum, making a point of never being alone with him.

Spencer continued to keep a close eye on her, watching from the sidelines and talking to Joe or Hank when she finished her twice-daily sessions with Indigo.

As for the Thoroughbred, Indigo was making definite progress. Each day he'd greet her with a welcoming whicker, and during the schooling sessions he seemed eager to please.

After each session she would take him out to the small track where a practice starting gate had been set up, hoping, as his trust in her deepened, to convince him that as with the horse box, he had nothing to fear from the metal contraption.

Using the same tactics as before, she walked him toward the starting gate, but from the opposite direction. He became nervous, sidling sideways and shying away, but Maura persisted, continuing to walk him past the hated metal device, talking to him all the while.

After half a dozen passes Indigo began to realize she didn't intend to lead him into the gate. On the last pass she changed tactics, this time stopping at the gate for several seconds before continuing on, allowing Indigo a chance to look at the contraption at close quarters.

She patted him and praised him, assuring him that all was well. She repeated the exercise, varying the approach, changing direction and stopping longer each time, managing on more than on occasion to have Indigo brush against the metal. To her relief and encouragement, his reaction was minimal.

Although she was well aware that race day was drawing closer, she refused to rush the process, confident that being patient with Indigo, taking it one day at a time, would be the key to success.

Maura continued these sessions until she felt confident Indigo had grown accustomed to and had even become bored with the gate.

On Thursday afternoon she instructed Joe to saddle and ready Indigo for a race, and she asked Phil, his jockey, to join them at the practice track.

This time with Phil riding Indigo, Maura led horse and rider toward the starting gate. Indigo was decidedly more alert, as if he knew that by having Phil on his back, things were different.

She'd told Phil of her plan to lead Indigo directly

up to and into the gate. And once Indigo was inside she'd instructed Joe to immediately release the mechanism to open the gate, allowing Phil and Indigo to continue through and out the other side.

In a testimony to the level of trust Maura had established with Indigo, he appeared calm and unperturbed as she led him into the starting gate. Phil gently nudged him forward and walked him out the other side with only the steady flick of his tail as indication he was in any way nervous or afraid.

Maura had been hard-pressed to hide her elation, but while she quietly accepted Joe's and Phil's congratulations, she cautioned them that the victory was only a small one.

Pleased with this breakthrough and wondering if Spencer was lurking somewhere nearby watching, she'd quickly scanned the track. There was no sign of Spencer, and Maura silently told herself she was a fool to feel disappointed.

They repeated the process several more times, leaving Indigo in the gate a few seconds longer each time. After more than a half dozen uneventful walkthroughs Maura told Phil to take him for a gallop around the track.

She watched Indigo's long strides eat up the track, and when Phil completed the circuit and brought Indigo to a halt, they were all smiling.

Maura asked Phil to join them again in the morning and told Joe to arrange to have a few more horses and riders available as an added distraction for Indigo.

By adding more horses and jockeys to the mix, she hoped at the very least to generate a situation more in keeping with a real race.

Leaving Joe to return Indigo to his stall, Maura made her way through the yard. Reluctant to return to the house for fear of running into Spencer, she headed instead toward the stable where the mare Stardust was housed.

Spencer had told her she could take Stardust out whenever she wanted. Suddenly the idea of riding out to the lake had great appeal.

Gerry, one of the stable hands, appeared as she entered.

"Would it be all right if I took Stardust out for a while?" she asked as she approached the mare's stall.

"No problem," he replied. "I'll saddle her for you. She could use a bit of exercise. Isn't that right, girl," he added, his tone affectionate, as he slid open the stall door.

Stardust seemed pleased at the prospect of an outing. The spring day had been sunny and warm, but now the air was cooling a little as the sun made its slow descent.

"Thanks, Gerry." Maura swung into the saddle. "If anyone asks, I'm heading to the lake. I think I can remember the way. Mr. Diamond took me out there when I first arrived."

"All right, miss," Gerry said before retreating.

Stardust, no doubt glad to be free of the stables for a while, broke into a canter.

Once out in the open countryside, Maura felt her spirits lift measurably. Horses and riding had been part of her life from as far back as she could remember. Her mother had been a house cleaner for the owner of one of the local stud farms dotted around the Lexington area.

Since her mother had been unable to afford a baby-sitter, Maura had always accompanied her to the job. Under the threat of a spanking, Maura had been instructed to stay in the kitchen and sit at the table and draw until it was time to leave.

Left alone while her mother worked upstairs, Maura had quickly become bored. She'd decided to explore, and once outside she'd made a beeline for the stables.

After wandering around unnoticed, she'd climbed through a narrow opening into one of the horse stalls. Tired from her efforts and totally unafraid of the big brown horse occupying the stall, she'd fallen asleep on the straw.

When they found her an hour later, Henry Wainright, the owner, took a shine to Maura and suggested that while her mother cleaned, Maura was welcome to help his eight-year-old son with his stable chores.

Her mother had been relieved Maura's antics hadn't resulted in her losing her job, and as for Maura, her love of horses had been born that very day.

Maura slowed Stardust to a walk as she drew near the lake. Not for the first time she admired the picturesque landscape and tried not to think of Spencer and the kiss they'd shared.

With a sigh she turned her thoughts away from Spencer to her father. She hadn't seen him since the evening Spencer had taken her to dinner in town, the night he'd danced with her, the night he'd kissed her.

Muttering under her breath for letting her thoughts drift back to Spencer, Maura reined in Stardust near the spot they'd stopped before. Dismounting, she secured Stardust to the branch of a shady elm and walked to the lakeshore.

A warm breeze fanned her face as she made her way to where an old fallen log lay partially buried near the water's edge. Sitting down, she removed the wide-brimmed Stetson Nora had insisted she borrow. She set it down next to her on the log and, reaching back, gently tugged the pins from her hair before shaking it loose.

Her scalp tingled and she moaned softly. Closing her eyes she held her face up to the sky, letting the breeze gently riffle her hair.

After a few minutes she opened her eyes to stare into the crystal-clear water of the lake. She felt hot and sticky after the ride, and the water looked cool and inviting.

Suddenly she remembered Spencer's teasing comments about skinny-dipping. A quick glance around the quiet haven revealed that she and Stardust were quite alone. The lake was on private property, and other than Gerry the stable hand, no one knew where she was.

Before she had time to think twice, Maura began unbuttoning her shirt. In a matter of minutes she was naked except for a pair of black bikini underpants.

She piled her clothes neatly on the log, and after another quick look round she removed the last stitch of clothing and ran toward the water.

It was colder than she'd expected yet strangely exhilarating and decidedly erotic. The water was shallow at first but it gradually deepened. As Maura waded in she scooped up handfuls and spilled the water over her breasts.

Her skin tingled, her breath caught and she shivered, though not from the cold. When the water reached the top of her thighs she sank down, totally submerging herself in its cool, wet embrace.

She broke the surface smiling as she silently acknowledged Spencer was absolutely right, the experience was not to be missed. Wiping water from her face, she dropped her head, letting her hair spread out behind her in dark coppery ribbons.

The water felt like silk on her skin and seemed to soothe her very soul. With a sigh of contentment, she floated like a leaf on top of the water, gazing up at the blue sky.

"I see you took my advice, after all."

# Chapter Nine

Maura instantly recognized Spencer's deep, masculine voice. She gasped in shock and her face slid beneath the water. She started to choke.

Arms flailing, she splashed around trying to get her footing. When her toes touched the sandy floor of the lake, she pushed up out of the water, coughing and spluttering and fighting for breath.

Tossing her wet hair out of her face, she glanced around in search of Spencer and spotted him, leaning against a tree trunk not far from where her clothes lay on the log.

"Very nice." He grinned at her, and instantly Maura realized her mistake. Crossing her arms over her naked breasts, she sank down until the water level reached her shoulders.

"I'm sorry. Did I startle you?" Spencer's tone was far from apologetic and she clenched her teeth, wishing now she hadn't acted so impulsively and decided to skinny-dip.

"Of course you startled me," she told him angrily. "I'll thank you to turn around and go back where you came from," she ordered.

Even from her crouched position in the water Maura could see the glimmer of deep amusement and something more, dancing in his eyes. A shiver tore through her, and she hugged herself tighter, not at all sure her reaction had anything to do with the cool water.

"I'd like to get out now," Maura continued.

"Need any help?" Spencer asked, enjoying himself immensely. He'd been on his way back from town when he'd spotted her riding Stardust in the direction of the lake.

"That won't be necessary, thank you," she replied curtly.

"I really don't mind," he teased. Her alabaster-white shoulders peeked out of the water, tantalizing him. And below the clear surface of the lake he could make out the curves of her naked body—a body he'd been openly admiring only a few seconds ago.

"But *I* do," she replied, with more than a hint of exasperation in her voice.

"I know! I'll stand guard," he offered, still smiling. "Just in case anyone else should decide to drop by."

"You're too kind." Maura replied, trying hard not to smile in response to the laughter lurking in his voice. Silently she had to admit that if their roles had been reversed she would have done exactly the same.

"No problem," Spencer said.

The moment he turned his back, Maura stood up and began wading out of the water. Once ashore she scrambled toward the log, ignoring the stabbing pain in her feet inflicted by the rocks.

She darted a concerned look in Spencer's direction. He hadn't moved. Grabbing her cotton shirt, she hastily dried the worst of the moisture from her body. The fact that she was cold and still damp made putting on her bra and panties more difficult than usual.

Once that was accomplished she reached for her jeans. She thrust her right foot into the leg and almost toppled over when it stuck halfway down.

She fell against the log, scraping her thigh. Muttering under her breath she tugged harder.

"Are you sure I can't be of assistance?" Spencer asked, obviously aware of her predicament.

Her heart beat a rapid tattoo against her breast as she darted him another glance. She'd expected to see him facing her, but to her relief he stood like a sentinel.

After a series of tugs and grunts she succeeded in pulling on her jeans. Grabbing her decidedly damp shirt, she put it on and with fumbling fingers began buttoning it.

"Are you decent?" Spencer asked. "May I turn around?"

"I'm decent," Maura replied.

Spencer slowly swiveled and felt his heart career against his ribs when his gaze came to rest on her. He supposed, if by *decent* she meant her body was covered, then she was right. But the way her shirt clung to her body outlining the natural curve of her breasts, *seductive* and *erotic* were more fitting descriptions.

He could recall quite vividly how her naked body looked when she rose like a goddess out of the water.

Moisture had cascaded over her shoulders, down her creamy-white breasts, slowing a little as it skimmed her flat stomach, before sliding into the dark valley below.

He swallowed, trying to alleviate the sudden dryness in his throat.

"Was I right?" he asked, his voice faintly husky as he walked toward her.

"About what?" She kept her gaze averted, knowing full well what he was talking about, but choosing to concentrate on gently squeezing water from her hair.

Spencer's low chuckle sent her pulse scooting into overdrive. He came to a halt in front of her. "Admit it. There's nothing quite like it, is there?"

Her breath hitched as she met his gaze. He was absolutely right. There was nothing to match her body's instant response his very presence seemed to draw so effortlessly from somewhere deep inside her. Every nerve tingled to life, every cell vibrated, waiting, wanting.

"No, there's nothing quite like it." Her voice sounded breathless, because she wasn't talking about the water at all. In fact she was remembering the last time they'd been alone together, when he'd kissed her until her bones had practically melted, and she suddenly wanted quite desperately to feel his mouth on hers again.

"What brought you out here? Playing hooky?" he teased.

"No, we'd finished for the day," she told him before dropping her gaze, fearful he might see the longing for him in her eyes. "I just wanted to be by myself for a while." She moved to gather up her socks, and sat down on the log to put them on.

"And I'm disturbing you. I'm sorry," he said.

Laughter threatened to break free, but she managed to stifle it. *Disturbing* didn't even begin to describe what he was doing to her.

"No problem," she assured him. She tugged on her boots and reached for her hat on the log nearby. "This is Diamond property, after all," she added, trying in some small way to distance herself from him.

"So, tell me. How did your session with Indigo go this afternoon?"

Maura heard the hint of worry in his voice.

"Good. Very good, in fact." She stood up and faced him once more. "He walked into and out of the starting gate without batting an eye."

Surprise and relief registered on Spencer's handsome face. He took a step closer, his eyes bright with excitement.

"That's the best news I've heard all day," he said with a smile.

"I wouldn't start celebrating yet," she cautioned, silently reveling in the fact that she was the reason he was smiling.

"But surely..."

"But surely nothing. Yes, Indigo is making progress. But with only one day left before the race I can't guarantee he'll behave on Saturday."

"I have a feeling you and Indigo will pull it off." He reached out and to grab a handful of her wet hair. "You'd better get back to the house. We don't want you catching a cold now, do we?"

The air between them was suddenly charged with tension. For a second, or maybe two, her heart forgot to beat. He was going to kiss her! She was sure of it.

Suddenly the silence was shattered by the sound of a telephone ringing.

Spencer cursed under his breath. Digging into the pocket of his jeans, he pulled out a small, black cellular phone. After a quick glance at the digital screen, he punched a button and put the phone to his ear.

"Hello?"

Maura turned and slowly released the breath she'd been holding, telling herself she wasn't in the least bit disappointed that he hadn't kissed her.

Not for the first time she reminded herself that he didn't trust her, that she was there to help Indigo. Besides, Spencer Diamond was way out of her league.

He wasn't remotely interested in her romantically. He was merely using his charm and good looks to try to find out why she'd really come to Kincade.

She sighed. What would his reaction be, she wondered, if she told him she was his wife's half sister?

Maura had thought about Lucy a lot during the past week. She'd hoped Nora or Elliot might comment on their daughter-in-law, but since the first night at dinner Lucy's name hadn't come up again.

Much as Maura wanted to ask about her half sister, she'd decided against it, sure Spencer would read something more than casual interest into her questions.

She could only surmise that the reason they rarely spoke of Lucy was out of respect for Spencer, who was obviously still grieving for his wife.

"Yes, Michael, we're still on for tonight." She heard Spencer say.

Maura froze. Could he be talking to her father? Was Michael coming to the ranch tonight? She held her breath, trying to contain the excitement sprinting through her at the thought of seeing her father again.

"I'm looking forward to it. Yes, I'll tell her. Bye." Spencer concluded the call and returned the phone to his pocket.

Maura waited for Spencer to speak, to explain, but he said nothing. She sensed he was waiting for her to ask him if his caller was Michael Carson. She refused to fall into the trap.

"I'd better head back," she said, making a move to where Stardust stood patiently waiting.

"Michael says hello," Spencer said.

Maura turned. "I'm sorry?"

Spencer's mouth curved into a smile that didn't reach his eyes. "That was Michael Carson. He said to say hello. I'm seeing him later."

"He's coming over?" Maura's question was out before she could stop it.

Spencer's eyes narrowed, and he shook his head. "No I'm having dinner with him tonight in town. He has a friend he wants me to meet, someone interested in moving a horse to the Diamond Ranch."

"Oh, I see." Maura managed a smile. Tugging the reins free she quickly mounted Stardust. "Have a nice evening."

"Thank you. I'll see you at Indigo's training session tomorrow morning."

"Fine," she replied, before turning Stardust in the direction of the ranch.

To Maura's relief and Spencer's elation, the morning session with Indigo went like clockwork. First Maura put him through his regular routine, then gave him a trial run through the starting gate. He performed beautifully.

Next Joe brought out the other horses and riders. Indigo's reaction to their presence was minimal. They were, after all, his stable pals. With the other riders milling around the track Maura led Indigo in and through the starting gate.

She continued this exercise, making him stay a little longer in the gate each time. After half a dozen walk-throughs, she felt confident that her patience and persistence had paid off.

"Incredible!" Spencer grinned at her as she crossed the track to where he'd been watching the entire procedure.

Phil and Indigo and the other horses and riders were headed around the track. "I don't know how to thank you," Spencer went on as they began walking toward the center courtyard.

Maura smiled, warmed by the sincerity in his words. "I'm still a bit worried about tomorrow," she confessed. "This setup isn't a patch on all the hoopla and noise and crowds that's part of a real race. I'd like to come along tomorrow, if that's all right."

"Of course you're coming to Santa Anita with us tomorrow. You're Indigo's lucky charm, and you'll be mine too, if he pulls off a win," Spencer replied. "Oh…I assume Mother did tell you she's having a prerace party tonight?"

"Yes, she did, but I don't think…" she began shyly.

"You can't stay in your room, if that's what you're thinking," Spencer teased. "If you hadn't called with your offer of help, Indigo would undoubtedly be facing disqualification tomorrow."

"I'm glad I could help," Maura said as they reached the first row of stables.

"Why don't you take the rest of the afternoon off?" Spencer suggested. "Go into town and explore a little. After all the work you've put in this week, you deserve a break. You're welcome to borrow one of the cars," he added as they arrived at the security gate.

"Thanks, but I don't drive," Maura replied. Never having been able to afford a car she hadn't bothered to learn.

Spencer glanced at his wristwatch. "I'd drive you into town myself, but Kyle Masters, our local vet, is due to arrive any minute. He's coming to give Indigo a prerace check and to take a look at Mystic Mountain's bruised hind leg."

"That's all right," Maura replied as they approached the steps leading to the verandah.

Spencer halted and turned to face her. "Look, I'm heading over to Michael's a little later. I could drop you off in town," he suggested.

At the mention of her father's name, Maura tensed. It was a reaction she couldn't seem to control, and she knew by the way Spencer's eyes suddenly narrowed that he'd noticed it too.

"It happens every time," Spencer said, the warmth in his voice quickly evaporating.

"What does?" Maura asked with a frown.

"Every time Michael's name is mentioned you react, your pupils dilate, you immediately tense up."

Maura felt a telltale blush suffuse her face.

"You're imagining things," she replied, astonished that he'd been keeping track of her responses.

"I wish I was." Spencer's jaw tightening. "I asked Michael last night if he knew you, if he'd ever met you before, if he knew why you would be so interested in him."

Maura swallowed. "And he told you he's never set eyes on me before. Am I right?" She challenged.

"Yes," Spencer reluctantly acknowledged.

"Don't you believe him?" Maura asked.

"Of course I believe him," Spencer replied, anger edging his tone. "But I also believe my gut feeling, and it's telling me there's something going on here, something you've been hiding from the minute you got here."

"Maybe you read too many spy novels," Maura said, attempting to lighten the tension arcing between them, but Spencer couldn't seem to let it go.

"Or maybe I know a lie or an evasion when I hear one," he replied.

"This is getting us nowhere," Maura said. Her connection with Michael Carson was none of Spencer's business, and until she talked to her father alone, she refused to acknowledge to Spencer—or anyone for that matter—that she was Michael Carson's illegitimate daughter.

She started to climb the stairs.

"Wait!" Spencer called. "I'm sorry."

His apology surprised her. She turned to look at him, to see if he was merely giving her lip service or if he was really sincere. She met his gaze and saw frustration, suspicion and regret in the depths of his blue eyes.

She sighed. "I'm not here to hurt anyone," she said softly, wanting to wipe the look of suspicion from his eyes. "You'll just have to trust me on that."

"Trust you!" He practically shouted the words at her. "Why should I? Maybe if you told me why you are so interested in Michael…"

Maura bristled. "It has nothing to do with you, and it's really none of your business," she told him, unable to control her anger.

"If it concerns my father-in-law then I think it is my business," he retorted. "He has lost both his wife and a daughter, my wife. When it comes to family, I'm all he has left, and I'm damned if I'm going to let anyone hurt him."

Suddenly she was strongly tempted to tell Spencer he wasn't the only family Michael had left, but she bit back the words. She admired Spencer's fierce loyalty to his wife's father, a testimony no doubt of just how much he'd loved her.

"If it will help," Maura said, "then you are right, I do have another reason for being here. More than that, I can't tell you. You'll just have to—"

"Trust you?" he finished for her, his mouth twisting into a sardonic smile.

"Yes," she replied, bravely meeting his gaze.

Their eyes held for several long seconds. Suddenly the silence was shattered by the sound of tires crunching on the gravel. They both turned to see a pickup truck round the corner of the house.

As the truck came to a halt beside them, Maura read the lettering on the door panel. Kyle Masters, Veterinary, Kincade, CA.

Spencer glanced back at Maura. "We'll finish this later," he said and before she could comment he turned and walked toward the dark-haired stranger climbing from the vehicle.

# Chapter Ten

Spencer hurried up the back stairs and down the hall to his bedroom. It was almost seven and guests were already beginning to arrive.

He was running late. He'd just returned from town, where he'd had a meeting with Justin Dubois, his father-in-law's friend.

He smiled to himself. Blue Diamond Ranch had a new client, and next week two three-year-old Thoroughbreds would be arriving to take up residence at the stables.

Closing his bedroom door, Spencer unzipped his jeans, tugged his shirt over his head and tossed it onto the bed. A minute later he stood under the shower's hot spray letting his thoughts drift over his busy but highly successful day.

To say he was pleased with how the day had gone would be an understatement. Watching Maura lead

Indigo into the starting gate that morning had done his heart good, and he silently acknowledged she'd done a tremendous job.

His thoughts lingered on Maura, recalling vividly their rather heated conversation just prior to Kyle's arrival.

When she'd started talking about trust...he'd nearly lost it. He'd gained one small victory. She'd confirmed she did have another reason for coming to California. But her calm refusal to explain further had once again left him frustrated.

But what had caught him totally off guard had been how much he'd wanted to say yes when she'd asked him to trust her.

Kyle's arrival had been timely indeed. Trust wasn't something Spencer was ready or willing to give, not to Maura, not to any woman for that matter.

He'd trusted Lucy, deeply, implicitly. Wasn't that what marriage was all about? But the vows they'd spoken on their wedding day had obviously meant nothing to his new bride.

Spencer pushed his morbid and painful thoughts aside. He let the cold water plummet on his head and back in an effort to numb the pain. Rinsing off, he stepped from the shower. He didn't want to think about Lucy or her betrayal, not tonight.

Maura pinned a smile on her face as Nora introduced her to a couple who'd just arrived.

After exchanging pleasantries, Maura excused

herself and retreated once more to a quiet corner of the living room. She wasn't at all sure she was cut out for parties.

Earlier, when she'd mentioned to Nora that she hadn't brought anything suitable to wear for such an occasion, Nora had insisted on driving her into town to one of her favorite dress shops.

Maura had refrained from admitting that she wasn't in the habit of buying dresses and happily accepted Nora's suggestions and advice.

She'd fallen instantly in love with a cotton shirt-dress the color of sunshine. Nora insisted its simple yet classic style accentuated Maura's slender figure and showed off her hair color to dazzling effect.

Afterward, Nora had taken her on a tour of Kincade, and she found herself wishing she'd been this at ease with her own mother. When Nora had started talking about Spencer, Maura had wanted to change the subject, but instead she'd listened avidly to every small detail.

But when Nora had voiced her anxiety and doubts about Spencer ever marrying again, Maura could only speculate that Spencer was still very much in love with his wife.

Dragging her thoughts back to the party, Maura toyed with her glass of wine and scanned the small crowd in search of her father. She'd seen him arrive a little while ago and now he stood talking with several men on the far side of the room.

It was her objective to create an opportunity to chat to him. She planned to ask about his hobby of collecting pioneer memorabilia, then reveal her own interest in the subject in the hope of garnering an invitation to view his collection, and at that time ask him if he remembered her mother.

A movement caught her eye, and she glanced around to see Spencer standing in the doorway. Her heart gave a little jolt as she noted his hair, shimmering like burnt gold, was still wet from the shower.

He looked stunning in a pair of jet-black pants and a silk paisley waistcoat atop an open-necked white shirt. His gaze drifted across the room, and for a fleeting second their eyes locked.

A shiver of longing darted down her spine, and she watched his mouth curve into a smile, making her wonder if he somehow was aware of her reaction.

"So, Maura, how are you enjoying your stay at the Diamond Ranch?"

Maura's breath caught and she broke free of Spencer's hypnotic gaze to turn to her father.

"I'm enjoying it very much," she replied politely.

"Elliot was telling me you've worked a miracle with Indigo," Michael went on.

Maura smiled, silently wishing everyone in the room would leave and she could be alone with her father. There was so much she wanted to say...to ask.

"We'll have to wait till tomorrow at the race track to see if he's right," she said.

Michael laughed softly. "You're too modest," he teased. "I for one will be betting on Indigo to win."

"I appreciate your confidence." Maura found the exchange both sweet and bitter. She drew a steadying breath. "I hear you have quite a collection of pioneer memorabilia."

"That's right, I do," he replied easily. "It's been a hobby of mine for a number of years. My great-grandfather loved to tell stories about making the trek across the country to settle in California."

"Really?"

"I became fascinated with the history," Michael continued, obviously enjoying the topic. "Whenever I traveled, which I did quite often as part of my job, I attended local fairs and antique stalls and gradually began accumulating various items."

"What was your job?" Maura asked, wanting to find out more about this man who was her father.

"My grandfather was a master shoemaker, and he started up a small shoe factory in the San Francisco area." Michael smiled. "The factory closed down a number of years ago, but there are a few folks who wish we were still in business.

"My father was taught by his father, but unfortunately I wasn't born with the necessary skills for working with the leather. I was a much better salesman than a craftsman, and so I traveled across the country with my samples, trying to persuade stores to stock our handmade leather work boots and women's shoes."

"You must have done a lot of traveling. Didn't

you say you'd been as far as Kentucky?" Maura asked, enthralled by the tale and understanding now how her father had come to be in Bridlewood and at the fair where he'd met her mother.

Michael nodded. "Yes, I did get as far as Kentucky," he replied. "You're from the Lexington area. Is that right?"

"Yes, a small town called Bridlewood," Maura said, and watched his face for any reaction. "It's about thirty miles east of Lexington."

"Bridlewood." Michael repeated, and Maura caught a flicker in his eyes as if the name triggered a memory. "I've been to Bridlewood," he said.

"I know," Maura replied, unable to stop herself.

"You know?" Michael was frowning. "I don't understand."

Maura instantly regretted her comment. "I'm sorry—"

"No, please, tell me. What do you mean when you say you know I've been to Bridlewood?" Michael insisted.

Flustered and annoyed at her slip, she tried to brush his question aside. "I shouldn't have said anything. I should have waited—"

"Waited? Waited for what?" Michael asked with a frown. He studied Maura. "Spencer asked me the other day if I knew you, if I'd met you before. I know we've never met, but there is something familiar about you...something I can't quite put my finger on."

Maura darted a nervous glance over Michael's

shoulder in time to see Spencer making his way toward them.

Fearful she wouldn't get another chance to talk to Michael, that this might be her only opportunity, she brought her gaze back to her father.

"Do you remember a woman named Bridget Murphy?" she asked, urgency in her tone.

"Bridget? Did you say Bridget Murphy?" Michael's eyes were wide with surprise. "Yes, I knew Bridget, but I don't understand.... How do you know Bridget?"

"She was my mother," Maura replied. "I'm her daughter...your daughter."

The words were out, and she watched as the blood drained from her father's face. He stared at her in shock and disbelief.

He shook his head in denial. "There must be some mistake," he muttered, though Maura could see the questions and the hesitation in his eyes.

"I'm sorry," Maura hurried on wishing now she'd never spoken. "I didn't want to tell you like this...I wanted to talk to you alone...."

"Is everything all right?" Spencer asked as he joined them. His gaze darted from Michael to Maura, aware of the tension in the air. "Michael, are you ill? You look pale." Concern for his father-in-law gave an edge to his voice, and he threw Maura an accusatory glance.

Michael didn't appear to hear Spencer. He kept staring at Maura. "Dear God! Is it true?" His voice was a hoarse whisper. Before Maura could respond Michael moaned and clutched his chest.

Frightened and appalled at what she had done, Maura instinctively reached out to him, but Spencer brushed her aside and put his arms around Michael.

"I think we should call an ambulance," Spencer said, keeping his tone even as he helped Michael to a nearby chair.

"No. I'm all right. I don't want a fuss," Michael said. He smiled in an attempt to reassure them.

"You don't look all right," Spencer commented crouching in front of him.

"Maybe we should take him to the hospital," Maura suggested, concern for her father overriding everything.

She doubted she'd ever forget the look of surprise she'd seen on his face when she'd spoken her mother's name. Why hadn't she waited to talk to him?

"I agree," Spencer said.

"Is something wrong?" Nora asked as she joined them.

"No, everything's fine," Michael insisted. "I'm getting one of my migraines, that's all," he explained. "I think I'll go home."

"I'll drive you," Spencer said.

"I'll go with you," Maura added.

Spencer threw Maura a withering glance. "I don't think that's necessary," he said helping Michael to his feet.

With a minimum of fuss Spencer ushered Michael

from the room. Ignoring Spencer's comment and unwilling to let her father out of her sight, Maura followed Spencer to his car.

"You are taking him to the hospital, aren't you?" she asked, once Michael was seated in the passenger seat.

"Yes." Spencer began to walk to the driver's side.

"I'm coming with you," Maura responded and before he could protest or argue she climbed into the back seat.

The trip to the hospital was made in relative silence. Spencer kept glancing at the man beside him, but Michael appeared to be deep in thought.

A quick look in the rearview mirror revealed Maura's concerned features, and not for the first time he wished he knew what she'd said to upset Michael.

When he'd first glimpsed Maura across the room, the urge to go to her, to take her in his arms and taste again the sweetness of her lips had been strong.

She'd looked like a ray of sunshine in her bright yellow dress, with her hair free of its usual confines, falling like coppery ribbons over her shoulders.

He'd seen Michael join her, and moments later they appeared to be chatting amicably. He'd started to cross the room to join them, but his mother had commandeered him, asking him to open another bottle of wine.

A few minutes later he'd thought to look their way again. This time their body language had spoken louder than words. He'd known something was wrong, and when Maura glanced up, he'd caught the look of guilt and panic on her face.

When he reached them Michael had looked like he'd seen a ghost. What could Maura have said that would have had such a startling effect on Michael?

Whatever it was, he intended to find out.

"I don't think this is necessary," Michael said twenty minutes later as Spencer and Maura walked him into Kincade Hospital's emergency area.

Once inside, a nurse came forward to meet them.

"Mr.Carson. Mr. Diamond. Can I help?" the nurse asked.

"My father-in-law is having some discomfort in his chest and we thought it best to bring him in," Spencer said.

"Wait here. I'll bring him a wheelchair." The nurse disappeared, returning with the promised wheelchair. "Have a seat, Mr. Carson."

"I'm feeling much better," Michael said, managing a smile.

The nurse smiled. "You're here now. Why don't we just take you through and have a doctor examine you? It's not very busy at the moment. It won't take long," she assured him.

"Very well," Michael replied as he sat down in the chair.

"The waiting area's on your right," the nurse said. "I'll know where to find you."

Maura nodded, but she stood unmoving until the

nurse wheeled her father out of sight. Tears stung her eyes, and she hurriedly blinked them away, not wanting Spencer to see them.

Her father hadn't spoken a word throughout the drive to the hospital, and Maura wasn't sure what to read into that. She'd thought after her revelation he would be asking her questions, or at least inquiring after her mother. He'd done neither.

Perhaps he hadn't wanted to say anything in front of Spencer. Maybe he didn't believe her, and by remaining silent he'd already given her his answer.

Pain sliced through her at the thought that her father may well have rejected her a second time. She leaned over as if she'd been punched in the stomach.

"Are you all right?" Spencer's question startled her, and she quickly straightened. She crossed the hall to the empty waiting area.

Maura sank down on one of the chairs, feeling defeated and dejected. A tear trickled down her cheek, and she hastily wiped it away.

"What did you say to upset Michael?" The question came from Spencer, who stood over her like a lion over its prey. "And don't tell me it's none of my business," he hurried on. "Michael is my business. I want answers. I think it's time you told me what this is all about."

Spencer watched as Maura lowered her face onto her hands and began to cry. Her shoulders started to shake, and soon her whole body joined in.

Stunned, he knelt in front of her and without a second thought hauled her out of the chair into his arms. She tried to resist, but he was stronger. He held her tightly, murmuring words of comfort, waiting for the storm to subside.

When at last her sobbing ceased, he gently eased her away from him. He noticed a box of tissues on the table nearby and, grabbing a few, handed them to her.

She drew a ragged breath and blew her nose. Wet tears clung to her eyelashes.

"I'm sorry," she mumbled. "I don't know what came over me."

Spencer put his hand under her chin, urging her to look at him. "You didn't answer my question," he said, noting the bruised look in her eyes.

Maura sniffed. "I'm not sure it really matters any more," she replied.

"It matters to me." He spoke softly, surprised at the tenderness he felt toward her and the urge to kiss away the pain etched on her lovely face.

Maura inhaled deeply, then slowly released her breath, trying desperately to steady her thoughts as well as her heart.

Being in Spencer's arms again had felt a little like coming home, and it had helped lessen the pain of rejection tearing through her. Here in Spencer's arms she felt warm and safe...and suddenly she realized that her feelings for this man went far deeper than anything she'd ever felt before. She'd fallen hopelessly and desperately in love with him.

The truth hit her with a force that sent her reeling,

and she was glad Spencer was holding her or she might have stumbled.

She wasn't exactly sure when or how it had happened…just that it had…and that she loved Spencer Diamond with all her heart.

Maura drew a steadying breath. Tucking this new awareness in a secret corner of her heart, she bravely met his gaze. The concern she could see in his eyes was almost her undoing, and she had to fight back a fresh wave of tears. With a concentrated effort she pulled away and moved out of his reach.

"He's my father," she said after a lengthy silence.

"What?"

"Michael Carson is my father," she repeated.

"There must be some mistake." Spencer couldn't seem to grasp what she was saying.

Maura managed a weak smile. "That's what Michael said, too. But it's true. I'm sure of it."

"But how?" He shook his head and ran a hand over his face. "I don't mean how…I mean—"

"Michael spent two weeks in Bridlewood twenty-eight years ago, while he was traveling on business," Maura explained. "That's when he met my mother and they started…a relationship.

"My mother never talked about my father…I never even knew his name until recently. After she died, I found a journal she'd kept the summer she met Michael Carson. In it she wrote that they became lovers."

"That doesn't prove anything," Spencer replied.

"You're right, the journal itself doesn't prove a thing," Maura acknowledged. "But I also found a letter my mother sent to him at his address here in Kincade, a letter that was returned to her, a letter telling him she was pregnant with his child."

"There must be some mistake," Spencer said again.

Maura smiled, wondering why he found it so difficult to believe what she knew in her heart to be true.

"Tonight I asked Michael if he remembered Bridget Murphy, my mother.... He said he did. But, I should have waited—"

"For what?" he cut in, his tone aggressive.

"I should have waited until I could have talked to him alone," Maura replied. "Having someone tell you suddenly out of the blue that she's your daughter...well, it's not exactly the kind of news you'd expect at a party.

"But when I saw you coming toward us, looking like a bouncer ready to throw me out...I panicked," she hurried on. "I wasn't sure I'd get another opportunity, and so I just blurted it out," she said, regret in her voice.

"That would certainly account for the shocked look on his face," Spencer commented.

"I'm sorry," Maura said. "I know it was wrong..."

"So this was why you came to California?" Spencer asked. "To meet the man you think is your father?"

"Yes."

"But, why so secretive? Why didn't you just explain?"

Maura bit down on the inner softness of her mouth. How could she make him understand? Spencer had grown up in a loving family atmosphere, with a father and mother to nurture and guide him. How could she possibly explain that ever since she'd been a little girl she'd dreamed of having a father?

Her mother had refused to talk about her father, forbidding her to ask questions. Suddenly finding out he had a name, reading in her mother's journal how her father and mother met and fell in love, had been like a fairy tale come true.

At first she'd been afraid to check out the information, fearful it would turn out to be wrong.

But unable to ignore the possibility that she might have the key to finding her long-lost father, she'd made a few calls, calls that had quickly established the fact that a man named Michael Carson still resided at the address on her mother's letter.

From that moment on there had been no turning back. Though she'd constantly reminded herself that he'd never responded to the letter or bothered to contact her mother, she'd refused to give up hope, praying each night that he would welcome her with open arms.

"I'm not sure you'd understand…" She faltered.

"Try me," Spencer replied his tone encouraging.

Maura drew a steadying breath and met his gaze. She saw compassion and something else in his eyes, something she couldn't define. "It's so difficult...I don't—"

"Excuse me, Mr. Diamond," said the nurse.

Spencer cursed under his breath and turned toward to greet the newcomer. "Is Michael all right?"

"Mr. Carson is fine," she assured him. "But the doctor suggests he stay overnight, as a precaution."

"Did he have a heart attack?" Maura asked.

"No," the nurse replied. "It was more like an anxiety attack."

Maura closed her eyes with relief.

"He wants to see you," the nurse continued.

Maura's eyes flew open, and her heart started to drum a tattoo against her ribs. "He wants to see me?" she said, hope flickering in her heart.

But the nurse was looking at Spencer. "Ah...no. Mr. Carson specifically asked to speak to Mr. Diamond, alone."

# Chapter Eleven

Maura flinched as if she'd been struck. Spencer felt his heart contract when he saw the wounded look that came into her hazel eyes. Suddenly he realized just how much finding her father meant to her, and why she'd kept it a secret.

He watched her silently withdraw. Crossing her arms over her breasts, she turned away, her body language showing him all too clearly the pain and dejection she was feeling.

"I'll be right there," Spencer told the nurse, who nodded and retreated.

"Maura...?" he began tentatively, fighting the urge to take her into his arms and offer comfort.

"I'm fine," she said, her voice devoid of emotion. "You'd better go and see my fa— Michael," she amended abruptly.

Behind her Maura heard Spencer sigh.

"I won't be long," he said.

Maura held her breath and waited until the sound of his footsteps faded.

She let out a soft moan. Biting down on her lower lip, she managed to suppress the sob threatening to break free. She swallowed the lump of emotion lodged in her throat, knowing that if she started to cry again, she might never stop.

Her father had rejected her once more. Though she'd tried to prepare herself for this possibility, somehow in the face of it, the heartache was even worse than she'd imagined.

The knowledge that she could have saved herself from this pain by leaving well enough alone flashed into her mind. She could have chosen to ignore her mother's journal and let sleeping dogs lie.

But she knew without a shadow of a doubt that if she had to do it again, she would. She had no regrets. She'd met her father, the man she'd dreamed about ever since she was a little girl.

Maura brushed aside a stray tear and sat down in one of the chairs. Her thoughts shifted to Spencer, and her heartbeat quickened, remembering how right and safe she'd felt in his arms.

A warmth stole over her, and for a few moments her spirits lifted. Though she doubted he believed her story that she was Michael's daughter, he hadn't berated her or belittled her, he'd simply listened.

Sensitive to her pain, he'd offered a shoulder to cry on, giving comfort, even though he'd never really trusted her.

His kindness and generosity had overwhelmed her and were just two more reasons why she loved the dynamic, multifaceted man.

She also admired the fact that he was fiercely protective of the people he cared about. He would make a wonderful father, firm yet loving, the kind of father she'd longed for.

She'd never met a man like Spencer, and she knew that when she returned to Kentucky she would be leaving a part of herself behind—her heart.

But there was little point in staying, little point in subjecting herself to more pain and disappointment. Now that Spencer knew about her connection to Michael, he would undoubtedly feel awkward with her.

Suddenly she wished she didn't have to face Spencer or his family. But she'd never run away from anything in her life, and she wasn't about to start.

The big race was tomorrow. She'd agreed to accompany Spencer and his parents to Santa Anita to watch Indigo. After they returned to the Diamond Ranch, she would make arrangements to leave.

Pain squeezed her heart at the thought of never seeing Spencer or his teasing smile again, never again tasting the passion in his kisses.

It would have to be enough to know that she was capable of loving someone so deeply and irrevocably...even if he didn't return her feelings.

Spencer returned to the waiting area a few minutes later to see Maura holding a baby. A woman, no doubt the baby's mother, sat nearby, a three-year-old boy in her lap.

Maura was smiling down at the sleeping infant, gently rocking the baby, crooning softly.

Spencer's heart stopped beating for several seconds, before stumbling on. There was something so infinitely touching, so incredibly beautiful about a woman with a baby in her arms.

He felt tears sting his eyes and emotions clog his throat. Not for the first time he was reminded of the loss of the child he'd longed for.

Maura glanced up, and when she saw the look of abject sorrow on Spencer's face, her heart plummeted. She'd secretly hoped he might have persuaded Michael to at least see her and talk to her. It was not to be.

Rising from the chair, Maura spoke to the baby's mother before handing back the sleeping infant.

"Is Michael all right?" she asked as they walked back to the car.

"He's fine," Spencer replied, but offered no more information.

The journey back to the ranch was completed in silence. As they pulled up outside the ranch house, Maura saw that there were cars still parked in the driveway, an indication that the party hadn't yet ended.

"I'd appreciate it if you would keep this just between us," Maura said when Spencer turned off the engine.

"Fine by me," he responded as he climbed from the car.

"Oh...and would you give my apologies to your mother and father?" she added as they walked toward the steps. "I don't feel much like partying. I think I'll slip in the back door and head upstairs to my room."

"Maura..." Her name on his lips brought her to a halt at the top of the stairs. "I'm sorry. Michael just wants—"

"You don't have to explain. I understand completely," she said cutting him off. She didn't want to talk about her father, didn't want Spencer's pity. "Oh, and by the way, if all goes well with Indigo at the track tomorrow, I'll be heading back to Kentucky as soon as I can make the necessary arrangements." With that she turned and hurried away, before the tears filling her eyes could spill over.

Santa Anita Racetrack was a beehive of activity. The crowd was buzzing, the excitement building, as the time for the sixth race, the big race of the day, the Jane Vanderhoof Cup, drew near.

The sun shone brightly in an azure sky, and the crowd seemed in a festive mood, everyone, that is, except Maura. She'd spent a restless night, a night tormented by dreams of her father and of Spencer.

Elliot Diamond smiled as he ushered his wife and Maura through the milling crowd, up the stairs to the Turf Club, where they would have a bird's-eye view of the race.

Maura hadn't seen Spencer since the previous night. At breakfast there had been no sign of him, and when she'd asked, Nora had told her Spencer had already left, choosing to accompany the horse trailer transporting his two racers to the track.

Maura had made the trip with Nora and Elliot, learning on the way that Michael was being released from the hospital sometime that morning, but that he'd decided to forgo the trip to Santa Anita.

While she was glad to hear her father had suffered no ill effects from the night before, she hadn't been surprised at the news that he wouldn't be joining them.

"Kate! Marsh! What a lovely surprise," Nora said as they entered the Turf Club. "Kate, my dear, are you sure you should be here?" Nora added, her tone anxious.

"I'm feeling wonderful, and the baby's fine," Kate assured her with a smile. "I needed to get out of the house for a while, and Marsh suggested we come today and give our support."

"I don't suppose you brought Bree, did you?" Elliot asked, referring to his granddaughter.

"Sorry, Dad. Sabrina's at a friend's birthday party and sleepover today," Marsh explained.

"Oh...forgive me," Nora said turning to Maura. "I'm being rude. Maura, I'd like you to meet Marsh, our youngest son, and his wife, Kate. Marsh, Kate, this is Maura O'Sullivan from Kentucky. She's been working with Indigo, and today we'll see the results of her efforts."

Marsh grinned. "Ah...the lady who, according to my brother, can perform miracles." He offered Maura his hand.

"We'll see just how true that is in a few minutes," Maura said with a smile. "It's lovely to meet you both," she added, turning to shake hands with Kate.

Kate smiled.

"Nora tells me you only have two more weeks until the baby is born," Maura commented.

"And it can't come soon enough for me," Kate replied with a tired sigh.

"Or for me," Marsh added, moving to put his arm around his wife.

Kate Diamond, her eyes brimming with love, turned to smile at her husband. Maura felt a stab of envy. They looked so very much in love. How she wished...

"Hi! I see you all made it." The sound of Spencer's voice sent Maura's pulse into overdrive. She took a step back and watched as he hugged Kate then slapped his brother on the shoulder. "Hey bro...glad you could make it."

"Shouldn't you be down at the walking ring?" Elliot asked, glancing at his watch.

"That's exactly where I'm going, but I came to get Maura." He flashed her a smile.

"Is Indigo all right?" she asked thinking something must be wrong.

"He's terrific, and raring to go," Spencer assured

her. "I got you a special pass. Thought you might like to come down and wish him luck."

"Yes, I would, thank you," she said, touched by his thoughtfulness. She was a little nervous about how Indigo would behave. The noise and activity at the track was totally different from the ranch, and there was always the possibility he might regress to his old habits.

"We'll be back in time to watch the race," Spencer said.

Maura felt Spencer's hand at her back guiding her through the crowd. A tingling heat spread through her where he touched her, and she was glad he couldn't see the blush warming her cheeks.

Joe and Phil smiled as they reached the ring. "Hi, miss, Indigo's been looking for you," Joe said, and laughed as the big horse shoved him aside to greet her.

"Hello, Indy." Maura stroked the blaze on the Thoroughbred's forehead and gave his ear a scratch. "Well, big fella, are you going to behave and walk right into that starting gate?" As if in answer to her question Indigo nodded his head.

"I'd say you just got the word straight from the horse's...ah...mouth, so to speak," Spencer said with a chuckle.

Around them other owners and trainers were giving their jockeys final instructions. Maura stood back while Spencer talked to Phil Jackson.

She studied Spencer, taking in his handsome profile, memorizing every tiny detail, knowing it would be all she'd have to last her a lifetime. Her heart contracted. Would he marry again, she wondered?

Maura hoped he would, and already envied the lucky woman. She felt sure he'd want children, and knew he'd make a truly wonderful father.

Spencer gave Phil a leg-up. "Go get 'em champ," Spencer said slapping Indy on the rump. Phil flashed a cheery smile as he followed the other riders from the ring. "We'd better head back."

Maura nodded and turned away. They wound their way through the crowd abuzz with renewed excitement as the start of the prestigious Jane Vanderhoof drew nearer.

Suddenly the sound of the hornblower playing the call-to-the-post filled the air.

"There you are," Nora said when they joined the rest of the family a few minutes later. "How was Indigo?"

"He's primed and ready to go," Spencer answered. "Give me your binoculars, Dad. I want to see how he fares at the gate."

Maura moved to stand next to Kate. The scene was spectacular; the mountains in the distance a fitting backdrop.

"Are you worried?" Kate asked.

Maura managed a smile. "A little," she replied.

"Spencer has faith in you," Kate said.

"That's why I'm worried," Maura confessed.

Kate laughed. "I see."

"What's happening?" Nora asked. "Marsh?

Spencer? What do you see?'' their mother asked impatiently.

"The horses are down at the starting gate. They're being led into gates now,'' Marsh replied. "Indigo's the last one in...."

He was silent, and a hush seemed to fall over everyone as they held their breath in anticipation.

"He's in! No problem!'' Spencer all but shouted. "And they're off!'' he added, the words almost drowned by the roar of the crowd as the race got underway.

Kate leaned toward Maura. "You've done your part,'' she said with a grin. "Now it's up to Indigo.''

Maura nodded, refraining from adding that her job here was over. And while there was comfort in knowing that she'd succeeded with Indigo, it didn't make up for her failure with her father.

Outside, the crowd yelled its encouragement to the riders and horses. Maura watched as the tightly packed group of eight horses and their riders rounded the curve and headed for the finish line.

In the middle of the pack, Maura could just make out the colors, an array of blue diamonds on a white background, worn by Indigo's jockey.

Suddenly she felt a pair of hands on her shoulders, and she knew from the ripple of awareness that shot through her they belonged to Spencer. He'd handed the binoculars to his father and was leaning over trying to get a closer look.

The noise inside the Turf Club grew louder as the horses galloped toward the finish line. Maura's heart thundered in her breast like the hooves on the track, but it had nothing to do with the race and everything to do with Spencer's body pressing against hers.

"Go Indigo!" Marsh shouted.

"He's pulling ahead!" Nora yelled.

"Come on!" Kate added her encouragement.

"Look at him go!" Marsh said.

"He's going to do it! He's pulling ahead!" Spencer yelled, excitement and satisfaction in his voice.

Indigo galloped past the finish line a full length in front of his nearest rival and below them in the grandstand the crowd exploded with a cheer that echoed around the racetrack.

Cries of joy erupted around her and suddenly she was spun around and hauled into Spencer's arms.

Laughing and fighting for breath, Maura didn't struggle. She closed her eyes and held on, giving herself up to the glorious wonder of once again being held in his strong arms.

She savored the moment, locking it away with other memories of Spencer.

"You did it!" Spencer said slowly releasing her.

"Indigo, did it," Maura replied smiling up at him. "Congratulations! I'm—" she began, but before she could say more his mouth claimed hers in a kiss that seared her soul.

Maura responded instantly, pouring all the love in her heart into the kiss, a goodbye kiss, to the only man she would ever love.

"Hey, Spencer! Unhand the poor woman," Marsh said in a teasing voice. "Shouldn't you be heading to the winner's circle to collect the trophy and the prize money?''

Spencer barely heard his brother's voice. It seemed that each time he kissed Maura, the world fell away and he was tossed into a whirlpool of desire. This time was no exception.

There was so much he wanted to say, but not here. Reluctantly he broke the kiss and flashed his brother a grin. "I was just thanking Maura for all she's done. She's the one who worked a miracle with Indigo, making it possible for him to win one of the most important races of the season," Spencer said, his arm still around Maura.

Maura felt her cheeks grow warm, but as she tried to wriggle free, Spencer only tightened his hold on her.

"Spencer, dear, you're embarrassing Maura," his mother scolded. "You'd better run along and collect the trophy and the purse."

"All right," Spencer conceded. "Why don't I meet you upstairs in the owners' lounge? Marsh… order a bottle of champagne, will you?"

"Good idea. It's on you, right?" his brother replied.

"Of course," Spencer said with a laugh.

Marsh turned to his wife and ran his hand over her rounded tummy. "No champagne for you, darling,"

"Your son and I will have orange juice," Kate answered as she covered Marsh's hand with her own.

The sweet exchange sent a stabbing pain through Maura. She turned away and noticed that Spencer was also watching the twosome, and she glimpsed the yearning in his eyes.

"Is it a boy?" Spencer asked.

"We don't know," Marsh replied.

"Sabrina wants a brother to play with," Kate said. "I think it's a boy because I get kicked from morn till night. Marsh thinks it's a girl because I'm carrying the baby high." She grinned at her husband.

"Either way you're a lucky pair," Spencer said, and with that he turned and hurried away.

As the horses for the last race made their way to the starting gates, Maura accompanied the Diamond family to the owners' lounge.

Elliot led them to a vacant corner overlooking the track. A waitress appeared to take their order.

"So, Maura, how long are you staying in California?" Marsh asked once the waitress had gone.

Maura managed a smile. "Actually, I'll be leaving tomorrow."

"So soon?" Nora commented.

"There's really no reason for me to stay on. I've done what I came to do," she said.

"Why don't you take some time and have a holiday?" Elliot suggested.

"That would be lovely, but I have to get back," she lied. Besides, the more time she spent with these warm and wonderful people, the harder it would be to leave. "I can't thank you enough for your hospitality," Maura said, her tone sincere.

"Ah…here comes the champagne," Elliot Diamond said as the waitress approached.

"And talk about timing. Here's Spencer." Marsh rose to make room for his brother.

Maura ventured a peek at Spencer. Her pulse kicked into high gear when his gaze sought hers, and he flashed a heart-stopping smile.

"I'd like to propose a toast," Spencer said, once the champagne had been poured. "To Indigo for his power, his strength and his amazing speed. And to Maura, miracle worker!"

"To Indigo! To Maura!" they repeated, making Maura blush anew.

For the next little while conversation flowed. A few friends came by to offer congratulations, but with the last race over, the crowd soon began to thin out.

"I think we'll be off," Marsh said. "We'll see you all tomorrow at dinner, that is if the baby doesn't decide to make an early appearance."

"No chance of that," Kate said with a tired sigh.

They walked out into the afternoon sunshine and followed the folks making their way toward the exit.

As they reached the parking lot, Spencer turned to Maura. "Why don't you drive back with me?" he said. "I could use the company."

# Chapter Twelve

Maura's heartbeat quickened at the thought of spending time alone with Spencer.

"It can be a tedious trip when there's no one to talk to." Nora gave Maura an encouraging smile.

"Sure," Maura said easily.

"My car is this way." Spencer pointed toward the opposite side of the lot.

"Fine. We'll see you back at the ranch," Elliot said, and with a wave they continued to their car.

"Indigo ran a terrific race. What did the stewards say?" Maura asked, curious to know if the threat of disqualification had been removed.

"Just that he'll be under review for a while. Here we are," he added as he came to a halt beside his sleek black sedan.

"Thank you." Maura slid into the leather seat and quickly pulled the seat belt into place.

The scent of Spencer's aftershave lingered in the car, and as it swirled around assailing her senses, she wondered if she'd been wise to accept his invitation. But as Spencer slid into the driver's seat, she silently rationalized that this might be the last opportunity she would have to be alone with him.

In a matter of minutes they were out of the parking lot and heading for the freeway.

Spencer drove with confidence, and the powerful car soon began to eat up the miles. The afternoon sun was already low in the sky, and the pink splashes of color it left in its wake gave the promise of another bright day.

"Tell me about my father," Maura suddenly asked when the silence became too much to bear.

Spencer darted her a quick glance. "What do you want to know?"

"Anything...everything," she replied. "I know nothing about him. My mother never even told me his name."

"I wonder why," Spencer said.

"Probably because she was made to feel ashamed of being pregnant and abandoned. There were some folks in Bridlewood who looked down on us," she said.

"Perhaps she thought if she buried the past deep enough, if she never told anyone or spoke about your father, she could pretend it never happened, forget that she'd made a mistake," Spencer said.

Maura said nothing, pondering his words. What he'd described fitted her mother to a T. After her divorce from Brian O'Sullivan, she'd never spoken of him again. She'd gotten rid of everything that belonged to him, and she'd even gone as far as to inquire how she could reverse his adoption of Maura. In the end, after a great deal of argument with various officials, she'd simply let the matter drop.

"You could be right," Maura said at last. "But surely any relationship, no matter how brief or how long it lasts, how good or how bad it is, deserves at least to be acknowledged and remembered.

"Even if things don't work out and a relationship goes sour, isn't it healthier to try to deal with the pain and accept the fact that it was a mistake and move on?

"Everyone makes mistakes. The trick is to learn and to grow from our experiences, both the good and the bad. I was the result of that love affair," she went on, "and pretending it never happened is like telling me I don't exist."

Spencer could hear the pain echoing through Maura's voice...and for the first time he had an idea of what it must have been like for her growing up. Finding her father, meeting him face-to-face, had been a way for Maura to validate her existence.

Silently Spencer acknowledged that he, too, was guilty of trying to forget the past. He'd tried to bury his memories of Lucy, forget she ever existed.

Maura was right. Lucy had played an important part in his life, and he'd learned a valuable lesson. That counted for something.

Besides he hadn't been entirely blameless—he'd
made assumptions about Lucy and believed wrongly
that they'd shared the same goals and dreams.

It was time for him to put aside the bitterness and
anger and remember the good times, the happier
times. It was time to move on.

"I guess I'll never know," Maura said with a
sigh.

"Never know what?" Spencer asked.

"Why my father returned my mother's letter...why he never contacted her again," Maura
said. "Were he and his wife happily married?" she
asked.

"As far as I could tell, yes," he replied.

"And their daughter, Lucy...your wife...what
was she like?"

Spencer was silent for so long Maura wondered
if he'd heard her. She glanced at him and noted a
look of tension in his face.

"I'm sorry. You don't have to answer that," she
said quickly.

"No...it's all right," he said, and realized he
meant it. "Lucy was beautiful and fun to be with,
but she was also spoiled. Ruth and Michael loved
her very much, but she'd grown up always getting
her own way."

Maura heard a mixture of love and sorrow in his
voice and not for the first time felt a stab of envy
for Lucy, who'd managed to capture this man's
heart.

"I wish I'd met her, gotten to know her," she

said. "I always wanted a brother or a sister. Being an only child can get lonely at times."

"How did you find out about your father?" Spencer asked.

"I was clearing out some of my mother's things and came across a diary," she said keeping her tone even. "I didn't believe it myself at first, but it was all there in black-and-white."

"So that's really why you came here," he stated.

"Yes," she said. "I didn't want to cause any trouble. I only wanted to meet the man who was my father. Is that so difficult to understand?"

"No," he said.

"As a little girl I made up stories about him, about the kind of man I thought he was." She twisted her hands in her lap. "Finding out he was still alive..." She ground to a halt. "I had to come—had to see him..."

Spencer reached over and placed his hand on hers. The touch sent a shiver of awareness chasing through her. Her gaze flew to meet his and she was surprised to see understanding and something more, something she couldn't quite define, in the depths of his eyes.

"Let's go talk to him," Spencer said, returning his hand to the wheel.

Maura's heart missed a beat. "Do you mean Michael?"

"Yes," he replied. "Last night he was in shock. He's had the whole day to think about the past, about your mother, about everything. You did say he remembered her?''

''Yes, but...'' Maura broke off, astonished by his offer. ''You would do this? You'd take me to my father?''

When Spencer made a left turn into a driveway not far from the Blue Diamond Ranch, Maura guessed the road led to Walnut Grove, her father's house.

She was growing more nervous by the second. ''Are you sure we should do this? Arrive unannounced, I mean?''

''You have questions you want to ask him, don't you?'' Spencer brought the car to a halt in front of the colonial style house.

''Yes...but—''

''No buts,'' he said. Switching off the engine he turned to face her. ''Maura, only Michael can answer your questions.... Don't you think it's time you had the answers?''

Maura met his steady blue gaze and drew strength from the warmth and compassion she could see in his eyes.

''Yes, but I'm afraid....''

Spencer smiled and his hand came out to capture a strand of her hair. ''Come on red, you're not going to back out on me now, are you?''

The use of her hated nickname put an angry glint in her eyes, just as he'd intended. He wanted quite desperately to take her in his arms, kiss away the fear and the anxiety clouding her lovely features. But he'd have to wait...

"Don't call me—"

"Red, I know. But you look so beautiful when you're angry," he added, and before she could admonish him again, and because he could no longer resist, he kissed her.

The kiss was much too brief and did nothing to satisfy the need suddenly churning to life inside him.

"Once you're through here, you and I have some unfinished business to take care of," he went on. "I'll wait for you. Yell if you need me." Reaching past her, he opened the passenger door.

Maura drew a deep breath and climbed from the car. As she walked to the front door she could hear her heart drumming a tattoo against her breast.

She pressed the doorbell and listened to the melodious chime. For a fleeting moment she was tempted to run back to the car, but the door opened and her father stood before her.

"Hello, Maura," he said, a faint smile on his lips. "I'm glad you dropped by. Come in," he invited.

Maura stepped into the tiled foyer.

"Congratulations... I watched Indigo's race on television. He behaved like the champion he is," Michael said as he led her into a spacious living room.

"Yes, thank you," Maura said, too wound up and nervous to pay much attention to the decor.

"Please, sit down," Michael said, indicating the multicolored brocade sofa nearby.

She perched herself on the edge of the cushion. "How are you?" she asked.

"I'm fine, thank you," he replied politely. He sat down at the other end of the sofa and angled his body to face her. "So...where do we begin?" He flashed a tired smile. "Your mother...?" There was a question in his voice.

"She died a year ago," Maura said. "A month ago I found a journal she kept. In it she wrote about meeting you at the Bridlewood Fair...."

Michael nodded. "That's right. Bridget was a beautiful girl. I thought there was something familiar about you. And now that I know...well, you do look like your mother. You have the same glorious hair, the same sparkle in your eyes."

"Why didn't you answer her letter telling you she was pregnant? Why did you return it?" Maura asked, suddenly impatient to get to the heart of the matter.

Michael's smile was filled with sadness. "I never received her letter," he stated calmly.

"But you must have," she was quick to argue. "It was addressed to you at this address. Someone read it, because it had been opened, and whoever read it scrawled 'return to sender' on the envelope."

"It wasn't me," Michael said. "I never saw your mother's letter. My father must have intercepted it."

"But didn't you ever wonder? I mean...you must have known my mother might get pregnant...after all, you were lovers. Why didn't you get in touch with her?"

Michael sighed. "I did start a letter...but I never sent it."

"You did?" Maura said surprise in her voice.

Her father nodded. "Maura, I'm sorry about last night. I guess I couldn't take it all in," he said. "I spent most of the night and all of today thinking about your mother, and about you." He paused. "Would you let me explain?"

Maura nodded. She'd come a long way to hear what he had to say.

He was quiet for a moment as if gathering his thoughts. "I was already engaged to Ruth when I met your mother," he began. "I told Bridget that, right from the start. I also told her that my engagement was a business arrangement, a deal my father had made with Ruth's father.

"It was supposed to be a marriage of convenience—convenient for my father and Ruth's father, not for me. Ruth's father owned a leather factory. They made leather goods, purses, wallets and briefcases. They wanted to amalgamate the businesses. The marriage was supposed to cement the deal.

"I liked Ruth, we'd gone out together a few times, but I didn't love her...at least, not then. That came later."

He stopped, and Maura noticed the sheen of tears in his eyes.

"My father told me the merger was important," Michael went on. "I knew business was in a bit of a slump, that the company needed a boost. And I knew how much it meant to my father to keep the business going. I told him he could count on me. I was closing in on thirty, and it was time I settled down. I told him Ruth would make a good wife.

"It's what he wanted to hear," Michael said. "I was leaving the next day on one of my sales trips and he said he'd set the plans in motion.

"Meeting Bridget wasn't something I planned or expected. She was young, beautiful and a little bit wild, and she wouldn't take no for an answer." He smiled at the memory.

Maura silently absorbed this new information about her mother, finding it hard to reconcile Michael's description with the woman who'd raised her.

"I'd been gone two weeks when I got to the Lexington area. I noticed the posters about the local fair and decided to stop for the day.

"After I met Bridget, I stayed on and spent every day with her. But at the back of my mind was the promise I'd made my father.

"I explained everything to your mother, told her about the merger, about my father, about Ruth," he went on. "She laughed and said 'Mickey, don't worry. I'm not looking for a husband—I only want to have fun.'"

Maura frowned...after reading her mother's journal she hadn't been left with that impression at all. She'd practically memorized every line. Was it possible she'd misinterpreted her mother's words, read more into them than was actually there?

On reflection Maura couldn't recall her mother

having actually written that she was in love with Michael Carson. She'd just assumed that was the case, simply by the tone of the entries.

"I stayed two weeks, and when I left I gave her my address and told her if she was ever in California to look me up...." Michael continued. "We parted as friends, nothing more.

"When I returned home, the arrangements for my wedding to Ruth were well underway," Michael went on.

"My father never commented on the fact that my trip had garnered relatively few new orders, but I think he sensed something had happened. I can only guess that Ruth and I must have been on our honeymoon when the letter from your mother arrived.

"My father wouldn't have thought twice about opening my mail...." Michael's voice trailed off.

"And when the letter was returned to my mother, she probably figured out you'd married Ruth and moved away," Maura said, filling in the blanks.

"It's the only explanation I can think of," Michael said. "I'm sorry, Maura," he said. "I should have done more. I should have written to her. It was irresponsible on my part. But if I'd known your mother was pregnant—"

"But you didn't know," Maura was quick to point out. "What I don't understand is why she didn't just tell me all this. Why keep your identity a secret?"

"Maybe it was her way of protecting you," Michael suggested, sympathy and sorrow in his voice.

"Perhaps she thought it was best if you didn't know anything about me."

"I guess I'll never really know what she was thinking," Maura said.

"I'm afraid there's no going back," her father said. "But we can make a fresh start. I know it's too late for me to be a father to you, Maura, but is there any chance we could become friends?"

At his question tears filled her eyes and her throat closed over with emotion.

"I'd like that very much," Maura managed to say as a single tear slowly slid down her cheek.

"It's more than I deserve. Thank you," Michael said, his voice husky with suppressed emotion.

"I'm leaving tomorrow," Maura went on.

"So soon?" her father said, sounding disappointed.

Tempted as she was to say she would stay longer, she was feeling a little overwhelmed. She'd been in such a rush to confront him, to tell him she was his daughter, and now she needed time to ponder all that he'd told her.

"Yes," Maura replied. "May I write to you?"

Michael smiled. "I'd like that," he said. "And this time I promise to answer," he added, a hint of humor in his eyes.

"Maybe you'd like to come to Bridlewood for a visit," she suggested tentatively.

"Yes, I'd love to see Bridlewood again," Michael responded.

"Good." Maura stood up. "I'd better be going.

Spencer is waiting outside. He was kind enough to drive me here.''

''Spencer is one in a million,'' Michael said as he walked her to the front door.

Michael opened the door, and they stood gazing at each other for a long moment.

''Thank you, for everything,'' she said.

Her father smiled once more. ''Would you allow me to give you a hug?''

Maura felt the tears sting her eyes. She nodded, and when her father's arms went around her, she felt the healing begin. They stood silently holding on to each other for several long moments before drawing away.

''I'll see you before you go?'' Michael asked, and Maura noted the glint of moisture in his eyes.

''I'd like that,'' she managed to say. Turning, she walked to Spencer's car. The door swung open and she climbed in beside him.

Spencer said nothing as he pulled her seat belt into place. He put the car into drive, hitting the horn lightly when he pulled away. Michael waved in response.

Beside him, Maura looked totally drained. Much as he wanted to ask how the meeting had gone, he kept silent. He glanced at her a second time and saw tears trickling down her face.

Spencer cursed softly. He wished they weren't in the car. He made the turn onto Diamond property and immediately swung the car onto the road that led to the lake.

His parents were probably already home, and he doubted Maura wanted them to see her like this. Five minutes later he brought the car to a stop.

Through the trees the water glinted in the setting sun. His thoughts drifted back to the afternoon he'd seen her rise out of the water, naked and stunningly beautiful.

His muscles tensed at the memory. He switched off the engine and turned to her.

"Are you all right?" he asked softly, fighting the urge to haul her into his arms.

"Yes. I am," she said, and he was relieved to see the beginning of a smile curve at her mouth.

"How did it go with your father?" he asked.

She brushed at the wetness on her cheek with the back of her hand. "Fine...good...great..." she told him, her smile widening.

"Let's walk, shall we?" he suggested.

They climbed from the car and strolled toward the trees. "What did Michael say?" Spencer asked. "Did he give you the answer you were looking for?"

"In a manner of speaking," she replied.

"I'm glad," Spencer said, his tone sincere. "So, where do you go from here?" he asked.

"We're going to keep in touch," she said. "And I invited him to come to Bridlewood," she added as they followed the grassy path toward the lakeshore.

"He didn't ask you to stay?"

Maura glanced at Spencer.

"No," she said, but there was no anger or bitterness in her voice. "We both need time to adjust, time to come to terms with this, to accept what happened and to forgive."

"So you're leaving?"

"Yes. Tomorrow, probably, depending on the bus schedule." Frowning she turned to face him. "I would have thought you'd be happy to see the back of me, Spencer."

"Then you'd be wrong," he said softly. "Because it's the last thing I want."

# Chapter Thirteen

Maura blinked several times and frowned.

"I don't understand," she said, wishing her pulse would slow its sudden and frantic pace.

"I'm not sure I understand it myself," Spencer said, coming to a halt near the moss-covered log where Maura had piled her clothes the afternoon he'd come upon her skinny-dipping. "You drive me crazy."

Annoyance shimmered through her at the comment. "The feeling's mutual," she shot back. "But surely if that's the way you feel, why on earth would you want me to stay?" she asked, puzzled by the look she could see in his eyes.

"It's quite simple," he said evenly.

"Then I wish you'd explain," Maura countered, not at all sure where this was going.

"Maybe I'll just show you." Before she had time

to draw a breath, Spencer reached out and pulled her into his arms, bringing his mouth down on hers.

Maura's gasp of shock and wonder allowed him instant access to the inner sweetness of her mouth, a sweetness he hadn't known he'd been craving, until now. Her response, immediate and devastating, was more than he deserved and filled his heart with hope.

He plunged his fingers into her silky hair as he'd so often dreamed of doing and, cupping the back of her head, brought their mouths and bodies closer still.

Her breasts were pressed hard against his chest, sending his blood pounding through his veins and arousing a need that clawed at his insides.

Maura's world was spinning wondrously out of control, and she didn't mind a bit. This was where she belonged, here in the arms of the man she loved with all her heart.

Her quest when she'd come to California had been to meet her father, the man she hoped would help her come to terms with the past.

But the happiness she felt at having finally made peace with her father was nothing compared to the joy at finding Spencer. He was the only man who made her feel alive, the only man able to touch her soul, the only man who evoked in her a depth of emotion she hadn't known she was capable of feeling.

Slowly, achingly, he broke the kiss to stare into her eyes.

"Wh—" She stopped and tried again, finding it difficult to think when all she really wanted was to kiss him again, to taste the raw need, to feel the passion.

"What was that for?" Her voice was a breathless whisper.

"Because I needed to kiss you. Because I think I'm always going to need to kiss you," he said matter-of-factly.

"I don't understand."

Spencer laughed, the sound like a caress on her already-heated skin. "You keep saying that," he responded. "But I think you understand perfectly. Otherwise, you wouldn't have kissed me back."

He kissed her again, all too briefly this time. "Don't be shy, red," he went on. "Tell me the truth. You're in love with me, aren't you?" His voice wavered as he spoke.

Her pupils darkened ever so slightly, and he could feel the shock and the tension humming through her. Had his gamble paid off? He'd only realized just how deep his feelings ran as he sat waiting for her outside her father's house.

Somehow she'd crept under his guard, stealing his heart before he'd even had time to figure out it was missing.

He'd never known a woman like her. Beautiful and intelligent, proud and courageous, Maura had acted with consideration and discretion under trying circumstances.

In the wake of learning about her real father she

hadn't barged into Michael's life—she'd quietly gone about her business, mindful of the damage she could have easily caused.

"How? I haven't...you can't—" Maura's words came out in an incoherent string. "And don't call me red," she said, suddenly indignant.

"But I like calling you red," he told her. "Besides, it suits you. And once we're married I—"

"Married?" Maura's heart shuddered to a standstill. Surely this was some kind of joke. She remembered distinctly his mother saying that she doubted Spencer would marry again. "You can't be serious." She was dreaming. She had to be.

"I'm perfectly serious," he assured her, humor lacing his voice. "After all, marriage is a serious business. I made a mistake the first time around. This time I intend to get it right."

"A mistake?" Maura was frowning now. "Are you saying your marriage to Lucy was a mistake?"

His expression changed. "That's exactly what I'm saying," he confirmed.

"But...I thought you loved her."

"I thought I did, too," he answered solemnly. "I believed, foolishly, that Lucy and I had the same dreams, that we wanted the same things. I was wrong."

"But...what happened?" she asked, needing to know, still struggling to get a grasp on what was happening. She'd either lost her mind...or...

Spencer's smile this time was touched with sadness. He was silent for a moment, still grappling with what Lucy had done. "I've never told anyone this before. But when I found out Lucy had—" He broke off. He slid his hands down her arms to capture her hands.

With a sigh he met her concerned gaze. "When I found out she'd aborted our baby, a baby she'd never even bothered to tell me about, I knew our marriage was over."

Maura inhaled sharply, seeing the pain in his eyes. "Oh, Spencer, how awful. I'm so sorry." Her heart went out to him.

Spencer smiled and touched her cheek with the back of his hand. "We'll have babies, lots of babies..." he promised, a catch in his voice.

"We'll have..." she began incredulously. "Spencer wait! You've lost me." She felt as if she'd walked into the middle of a rehearsal for a play, only no one had given her a script and she didn't know her lines. "What do you mean, we'll have babies? You don't even like me."

Spencer shook his head. "That's not true. I do like you...I just didn't trust you. I knew you were hiding something, and that got in the way of everything.

"I wish you'd confided in me about Michael, but I understand why you didn't. And I can only admire you for the way you've handled everything. I've never known a woman like you. You're the most beautiful, most patient, most dedicated, most caring person I've ever met." He came to a halt. "Don't you get it!" He tugged her closer and brought her face to within inches of his.

He gazed into her eyes, seeing the confusion, the fear and the hope.

"I love you, Maura O'Sullivan," he said, his voice throaty with emotion. "I think I fell in love with you the night I met you in Kentucky, when I asked you to come to California and you told me what I could do with my invitation.

"And I fell a little deeper the day I kissed you right here by the lake. And deeper still when I caught you skinny-dipping—"

"You love me?" Her tone was incredulous, as if he'd told her pigs could fly.

"Dammit, red. I just said I did," Spencer said exasperatedly. "Would you put me out of my misery, please?" he begged. "Say you'll marry me. Say you love me. Say something." His voice wavered ever so slightly, and as she met his gaze she could see behind his teasing bravado a look of fear and vulnerability.

Spencer Diamond afraid, vulnerable? It hardly seemed possible. And she wouldn't have believed it if she hadn't seen it with her own eyes.

"Dear God, woman! Speak to me." Desperation edged his voice.

Joy exploded through her, and she smiled, her heart aglow with love. "Oh, Spencer…" She spoke his name on a sigh. "I do love you, I love you with all my heart. I was afraid to—"

Her words were silenced as his mouth claimed

hers in a kiss so tender, so achingly sweet, he stole her heart a second time.

His kiss deepened, igniting a response she was only too eager to give. Here in Spencer's arms she'd found her home...her family...at last.

Spencer reluctantly broke the kiss to forge a trail of kisses across her jaw to her ear. He kissed her earlobe then nibbled at the sensitive area below it.

"Spencer...do you know what you're doing to me?" Maura's voice was a husky whisper of desire. Her body was on fire, her skin aching for his touch, his caress.

"The same as you're doing to me, my love," Spencer replied, his breathing rapid, his heart racing. "Maybe we should cool off a little.... What about a dip in the lake...a skinny-dip, that is."

Maura's laugh was a little shaky. "That sounds very tempting," she said, straining closer.

Spencer groaned. "I want to make love to you, here, now." His tone was urgent, and when she felt his hand cup her breast, she gasped at the new and erotic sensation that spiraled through her.

"And I want you," she said with quiet desperation. "Only I haven't...I mean...I've never—" She ground to a halt.

Spencer instantly pulled away to look into her eyes, seeing the innocence shining in their depths. He framed her face with his hands. Was there no end to the surprises this woman had for him? "You're a virgin?"

Maura nodded. "Is that bad?"

"Bad?" Spencer repeated dumbfounded. He kissed her long and hard. "It's the most wonderful gift you could ever give, and after the way I've treated you, certainly more than I deserve." His tone was heartfelt. He sighed. "We'd better go before I lose my resolve."

"But, Spencer, I thought... Don't you want me?" She blurted out, suddenly unsure.

"Of course I want you," he assured her. "But when we make love for the first time, I want everything to be perfect for you, for us. I can wait...it won't be easy, believe me, but I can wait. Just don't make me wait too long."

"What about a June wedding?" she replied, and wondered what she'd done to deserve the love of a man like Spencer.

"June it is," he agreed. "And why don't we ask your father if he'd like to give you away," Spencer suggested.

Maura's heart swelled with love. She felt tears gather in her eyes. "I'd like that. I'd like that very much."

Spencer kissed her again, a soft delicate kiss that made her sigh.

"Let's go tell my folks there's going to be a new Diamond in the family."

# Epilogue

Maura Diamond looked radiant as she walked down the aisle on the arm of her brand new husband.

The bodice of her bridal gown was studded with pearls and the train flowed behind her like a snowy-white carpet. Outside the bright California sunshine greeted them along with a small crowd of locals.

As they waited for the rest of the bridal party to join them, Spencer turned to his wife.

"Michael looked so proud when he walked into the church with you on his arm," he said.

"He was shaking like a leaf…or I was, or maybe we both were," Maura replied with a tinkling laugh.

Her thoughts drifted back over the past six weeks. The days had flown by in a blur of activity. She'd made a quick trip back to Kentucky to arrange for her belongings to be transported west, then returned to California to become embroiled in the plans for her wedding to Spencer.

Her father had agreed to give her away, and over the past few weeks their tentative friendship had begun to blossom into a warm and loving relationship.

Maura had never known such happiness. For the first time in her life she was part of a real family, a family who accepted and loved her the way she'd always longed for and dreamed about.

She glanced at her husband, the man who'd made all her dreams come true, and sent up a silent prayer of thanks.

Spencer's brother Marsh and his wife Kate were the first to join them. They'd left their one-month-old son, Cole, at home with his nanny.

Next came Spencer's sister, Piper, who'd flown in from London only a few days ago. Since her arrival Piper had seemed a little withdrawn, and Maura had glimpsed a look of worry in her sister-in-law's eyes.

Elliot, Nora and Michael joined them, their faces wreathed in smiles.

"So what do you all think of the new family Diamond?" Spencer asked, grinning at his bride.

"A high quality Diamond, if ever I saw one," Elliot replied, making Maura blush.

"Shouldn't the limousine be here by now," Maura asked wanting to divert their attention.

"Oh...I forgot to tell you," Spencer said.

"Forgot to tell me what?" Maura asked, hearing the teasing note in his voice.

"I have a surprise for you," he said.

"Surprise? Spencer...what?"

"Your father helped arrange it," Spencer quickly explained. "Ah...here they come."

Maura turned in time to see a covered wagon, drawn by two horses and decorated with white ribbons, appear at the gate of the churchyard.

"Oh...how wonderful," Maura said, tears stinging her eyes. She turned to her father who stood nearby. "Thank you."

Michael smiled and leaned forward to kiss his daughter's cheek.

Spencer tugged at her hand. "Come on...let's get this show on the road."

With a little help from her father and her husband, Maura was soon seated next to Spencer at the front of the wagon.

She grinned as she tossed her bouquet into the crowd standing on the sidewalk. Spencer's sister Piper looked surprised when the flowers landed in her arms.

The horses started to move and as the wagon rolled forward Maura suddenly knew the feeling of wonder and excitement the pioneers must have felt, as they rode together toward their future.

*     *     *     *     *

*Don't miss the third and final story in the Diamond trilogy. When Spencer's sister Piper returns home pregnant and alone, she gets comfort and support from an unexpected source. Kyle Masters, the man she loved and left years ago comes to her rescue...but for reasons of his own. Can they put the past behind them and find true happiness at last? Watch for DENIM AND DIAMONDS this summer.*

**Silhouette** ROMANCE™

## One little...two little...three little...BABIES!

What are three confirmed bachelor brothers to do
when they suddenly become guardians to triplets?

Find out in bestselling author
**Susan Meier**'s new trilogy

**BREWSTER BABY BOOM**

**THE BABY BEQUEST**—On sale in January 2000
Evan Brewster needed baby lessons fast! And surprisingly, his
father's former assistant seemed to have the perfect knack with
the baby brood—and with Evan's heart....

**BRINGING UP BABIES**—On sale in February 2000
Chas Brewster was desperate to hire a nanny, but what was
he to do when he wanted Lily's involvement to become
much more personal?

**OH, BABIES!**—On sale in March 2000
Grant Brewster was known for his control—at least until Kristen
sneaked her way into his life. Suddenly the all-so-cool bachelor
was getting hot and bothered—and enjoying it!

Available at your favorite retail outlet...only from
**SILHOUETTE ROMANCE®**

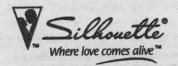

**Silhouette®**
*Where love comes alive*™

If you enjoyed what you just read,
then we've got an offer you can't resist!

# Take 2 bestselling love stories FREE!

# Plus get a FREE surprise gift!

*Soldiers of Fortune...prisoners of love.*

*Back by popular demand, international bestselling author* **Diana Palmer**'s *daring and dynamic* Soldiers of Fortune *return!*

*Don't miss these unforgettable romantic classics in our wonderful 3-in-1 keepsake collection. Available in April 2000.\**

And look for a **brand-new** *Soldiers of Fortune* tale in May. Silhouette Romance presents the next book in this riveting series:

# MERCENARY'S WOMAN

(SR #1444)

She was in danger and he fought to protect her. But sweet-natured Sally Johnson dreamed of spending forever in Ebenezer Scott's powerful embrace. Would she walk down the aisle as this tender mercenary's bride?

Then in January 2001, look for THE WINTER SOLDIER in Silhouette Desire!

*Available at your favorite retail outlet.*
*\*Also available on audio from Brilliance.*

# Silhouette
# ROMANCE™
# COMING NEXT MONTH

**#1432 A ROYAL MASQUERADE—Arlene James**
*Royally Wed*
Prince Roland Thorton posed as an employee of his family's royal
rival to find his sister's kidnapper, not to woo a lady's maid! But
one look at lovely Lily and he was hooked. Until he learned his
lady love herself was masquerading....

**#1433 OH, BABIES!—Susan Meier**
*Brewster Baby Boom*
When Kristen Devereaux discovered she was an aunt, she took a
job caring for her orphaned triplet nieces and nephew. Then she
met Grant Brewster—their sexy uncle and guardian—and resolved
to change her position from nanny...to wife!

**#1434 JUST THE MAN SHE NEEDED—Karen Rose Smith**
Cowboy Slade Coleburn never stayed in one place too long, but
when he saw pretty—and pregnant—Emily Lawrence running a
ranch by herself, he had to help. Before long, her home felt like
his...and her kisses like heaven. Loner Slade *couldn't* be ready for
"I do," could he?

**#1435 THE BABY MAGNET—Terry Essig**
Businessman Luke DeForest had a way with women, yet he was
clueless when it came to the two-year-old who had landed in his lap!
Luckily, kind and beautiful Marie Ferguson was willing to help. Had
Luke attracted the thing he'd thought he'd never want—a family?

**#1436 CALLIE, GET YOUR GROOM—Julianna Morris**
*That* was Callie Webster? The tomboy who'd had a crush on
Mike Fitzpatrick years ago? She'd grown up, and in her place was a
drop-dead gorgeous woman! Mike's mind saw the youngster he
remembered and said "no way." Too bad his heart—and body—
had other plans!

**#1437 WHAT THE COWBOY PRESCRIBES...—Mary Starleigh**
Just what the doctor ordered! Dr. Meg Graham needed a partner to
run her Texas clinic, when handsome Dr. Steve Hartly moved in—
right next door. Trouble was, he'd given up on medicine—and
women—altogether...until Meg showed him what he was missing.

CMN0300

# SILHOUETTE'S 20TH ANNIVERSARY CONTEST
## OFFICIAL RULES
### NO PURCHASE NECESSARY TO ENTER

1. To enter, follow directions published in the offer to which you are responding. Contest begins 1/1/00 and ends on 8/24/00 (the "Promotion Period"). Method of entry may vary. Mailed entries must be postmarked by 8/24/00, and received by 8/31/00.

2. During the Promotion Period, the Contest may be presented via the Internet. Entry via the Internet may be restricted to residents of certain geographic areas that are disclosed on the Web site. To enter via the Internet, if you are a resident of a geographic area in which Internet entry is permissible, follow the directions displayed on-line, including typing your essay of 100 words or fewer telling us "Where In The World Your Love Will Come Alive." On-line entries must be received by 11:59 p.m. Eastern Standard time on 8/24/00. Limit one e-mail entry per person, household and e-mail address per day, per presentation. If you are a resident of a geographic area in which entry via the Internet is permissible, you may, in lieu of submitting an entry on-line, enter by mail, by hand-printing your name, address, telephone number and contest number/name on an 8"x 11" plain piece of paper and telling us in 100 words or fewer "Where In The World Your Love Will Come Alive," and mailing via first-class mail to: Silhouette 20ᵗʰ Anniversary Contest, (in the U.S.) P.O. Box 9069, Buffalo, NY 14269-9069; (In Canada) P.O. Box 637, Fort Erie, Ontario, Canada L2A 5X3. Limit one 8"x 11" mailed entry per person, household and e-mail address per day. On-line and/or 8"x 11" mailed entries received from persons residing in geographic areas in which Internet entry is not permissible will be disqualified. No liability is assumed for lost, late, incomplete, inaccurate, nondelivered or misdirected mail, or misdirected e-mail, for technical, hardware or software failures of any kind, lost or unavailable network connection, or failed, incomplete, garbled or delayed computer transmission or any human error which may occur in the receipt or processing of the entries in the contest.

3. Essays will be judged by a panel of members of the Silhouette editorial and marketing staff based on the following criteria:

   Sincerity (believability, credibility)—50%
   Originality (freshness, creativity)—30%
   Aptness (appropriateness to contest ideas)—20%

   Purchase or acceptance of a product offer does not improve your chances of winning. In the event of a tie, duplicate prizes will be awarded.

4. All entries become the property of Harlequin Enterprises Ltd., and will not be returned. Winner will be determined no later than 10/31/00 and will be notified by mail. Grand Prize winner will be required to sign and return Affidavit of Eligibility within 15 days of receipt of notification. Noncompliance within the time period may result in disqualification and an alternative winner may be selected. All municipal, provincial, federal, state and local laws and regulations apply. Contest open only to residents of the U.S. and Canada who are 18 years of age or older, and is void wherever prohibited by law. Internet entry is restricted solely to residents of those geographical areas in which Internet entry is permissible. Employees of Torstar Corp., their affiliates, agents and members of their immediate families are not eligible. Taxes on the prizes are the sole responsibility of winners. Entry and acceptance of any prize offered constitutes permission to use winner's name, photograph or other likeness for the purposes of advertising, trade and promotion on behalf of Torstar Corp. without further compensation to the winner, unless prohibited by law. Torstar Corp and D.L. Blair, Inc., their parents, affiliates and subsidiaries, are not responsible for errors in printing or electronic presentation of contest or entries. In the event of printing or other errors which may result in unintended prize values or duplication of prizes, all affected contest materials or entries shall be null and void. If for any reason the Internet portion of the contest is not capable of running as planned, including infection by computer virus, bugs, tampering, unauthorized intervention, fraud, technical failures, or any other causes beyond the control of Torstar Corp. which corrupt or affect the administration, secrecy, fairness, integrity or proper conduct of the contest, Torstar Corp. reserves the right, at its sole discretion, to disqualify any individual who tampers with the entry process and to cancel, terminate, modify or suspend the contest or the Internet portion thereof. In the event of a dispute regarding an on-line entry, the entry will be deemed submitted by the authorized holder of the e-mail account submitted at the time of entry. Authorized account holder is defined as the natural person who is assigned to an e-mail address by an Internet access provider, on-line service provider or other organization that is responsible for arranging e-mail address for the domain associated with the submitted e-mail address.

5. Prizes: Grand Prize—a $10,000 vacation to anywhere in the world. Travelers (at least one must be 18 years of age or older) and parent or guardian if one traveler is a minor, must sign and return a Release of Liability prior to departure. Travel must be completed by December 31, 2001, and is subject to space and accommodations availability. Two hundred (200) Second Prizes—a two-book limited edition autographed collector set from one of the Silhouette Anniversary authors: Nora Roberts, Diana Palmer, Linda Howard or Annette Broadrick (value $10.00 each set). All prizes are valued in U.S. dollars.

6. For a list of winners (available after 10/31/00), send a self-addressed, stamped envelope to: Harlequin Silhouette 20ᵗʰ Anniversary Winners, P.O. Box 4200, Blair, NE 68009-4200.

Contest sponsored by Torstar Corp., P.O. Box 9042, Buffalo, NY 14269-9042.

# ENTER FOR
# A CHANCE TO WIN*

## Silhouette's 20th Anniversary Contest

### Tell Us Where in the World
### You Would Like *Your* Love To Come Alive...
### And We'll Send the Lucky Winner There!

Silhouette wants to take you wherever
your happy ending can come true.

Here's how to enter: Tell us, in 100 words or less,
where you want to go to make your love come alive!

In addition to the grand prize, there will be 200
runner-up prizes, collector's-edition book sets
autographed by one of the Silhouette anniversary
authors: **Nora Roberts, Diana Palmer,
Linda Howard or Annette Broadrick.**

## DON'T MISS YOUR CHANCE TO WIN!
## ENTER NOW! No Purchase Necessary

### Silhouette®
*Where love comes alive™*

---

Name: _____

Address: _____

City: _____ State/Province: _____

Zip/Postal Code: _____

Mail to Harlequin Books: **In the U.S.:** P.O. Box 9069, Buffalo, NY
14269-9069; **In Canada:** P.O. Box 637, Fort Erie, Ontario, L4A 5X3

*No purchase necessary—for contest details send a self-addressed stamped envelope to:
Silhouette's 20th Anniversary Contest, P.O. Box 9069, Buffalo, NY, 14269-9069 (include
contest name on self-addressed envelope). Residents of Washington and Vermont may
omit postage. Open to Cdn. (excluding Quebec) and U.S. residents who are 18 or over.
Void where prohibited. Contest ends August 31, 2000.

PS20CON_R